Leslie

MORGAN'S LEAP BOOK 2

KATHI S. BARTON

This is a work of fiction. Names, characters, places, and incidents are products of the author's imagination or are used fictitiously and are not to be construed as real. Any resemblance to actual events, locations, organizations, or persons, living or dead, is entirely coincidental.

World Castle Publishing, LLC
Pensacola, Florida
Copyright © Kathi S. Barton 2021
Hardback ISBN: 97819567880200
Paperback ISBN: 9781956788037
eBook ISBN: 9781956788044
First Edition World Castle Publishing, LLC, October 4, 2021
http://www.worldcastlepublishing.com

Licensing Notes

Cover: Karen Fuller
Editor: Maxine Bringenberg

Chapter 1

Leslie made his way to the side of the house, where the wraparound porch made the corner. Sliding to the floor, he stretched out his legs and let out a long slow breath. It wasn't as if he wasn't used to having the house at high decibels all the time. It was just too much with all the women and others there as well. When the door opened and closed at the front of the house, Leslie wondered if his mom was coming out to scold him or to join him. He was surprised to see Venetia standing at the railing, not five feet from where he was sitting.

"I'm remembering more and more all the time. There are a great many things I'd like to forget, but one I did want to share with you is that I knew that Betty and Sherman weren't my parents. They told me when I fell from the bleachers at school and broke my ankle. They didn't know any of my history." She looked at him. "Are you unhappy with me being your mate?"

"Not at all. Nervous? Yes, I'm that. But not unhappy. I was overwhelmed by all the noise in the place." She nodded as if she understood that as well. "Would you like to take a walk? I can show you around, and we can get to know one another."

"I'd love that." He got up and stretched. "You're very tall, aren't you? I was going to say large, but that's not all. You're in great shape and have good bones."

"It's the magic that keeps us trim. And the fact that we all work around here. I'll point out some of the things going on as we walk if you'd like." Again, she said that would be good. "We'll start this way. I've been craving an apple for most of the morning. Mom handed them out to your parents, which is good. I'm glad everyone is enjoying the fruits of our labors and—I'm babbling. I don't usually get all tongue-tied when I'm talking. I think it's mostly because you're so beautiful, and I want to make a good impression."

"You have. All of you have. I don't know my biological parents all that well, but they've been singing your praises since they arrived." They started for the woods as she continued to tell him what her parents were saying. "I like your mom, too. And Hanna. She's very intense, but I like her very much."

"She and Carroll are going to have a baby. We're all still trying to figure out how that is going to work." Venetia asked him what he meant. "We're the first shifters, and since we were made by two leopards, we've no idea if she'll have kittens that will shift or humans that will shift. But whatever they have, we'll all love them and protect them with our lives."

"I don't know you well enough to judge, but it's been my experience that people talk a big game and don't follow through on their promises." He said they would. "As I said, I don't know you well enough yet to say yes or no. I'm not trying to pick a fight with you, Leslie. I believe you when you say it, but humans aren't usually so good about following through on promises. You do know I'm a witch, don't you?"

"I do. I didn't until you found out, but yes. It doesn't bother me if that is what you're asking. In fact, I'm glad that if something—"

"Your lordship. You must go to the river. Now." He took off in the direction of the river after asking Venetia to please be careful. The urgency of Hale's voice had him running. Shifting to his cat so he could move faster, he arrived at the river's edge in record time. "There. See it?"

The car was upside down in the water. Shifting once again, he was able to roll the car to an upright position. It was then he saw the car had two children inside, with two adults in the front. Smashing one of the windows, which were all closed, he pulled the man out first.

"I can bring the car to the edge." Venetia did just that, pulling the car right out of the fast-moving water and onto the edge of the shoreline. "I'm sending the faeries up and down the river to see if there are any others around."

"Good thinking. Thanks." Coming out of the water, he was embarrassed slightly that he'd not thought to dress himself. As soon as he did, he laughed when Venetia's cheeks were as red as he was sure his were. "I didn't think beyond getting the people out of the car."

"That's fine."

The two of them pulled the people from the car. "Can you save them?"

"Yes. However, not the man. He's been

dead too long for me to be able to bring him back without consequences." Nodding, he pulled the smallest child — he thought her to be about six or seven months old — from the car seat and laid her on the ground. They realized the little boy was hurt badly after she was able to bring him back. "They were drugged. There is a great deal of something in their system. They would have not been able to survive had you not been warned. The poison in their bodies was lethal."

"Do you know what it was?" She said it was heroin. "All of them, or just the children? The reason I ask is, the man was shot in the head, and the gas pedal was pushed down. Also, and I have no idea why this just popped into my head when I opened the door just now, the lights came on, as well as the sounds. So I'm thinking they weren't in the water very long."

"I think you might be correct."

Leslie reached out to his family and let them know what was going on. The baby started crying but quieted down some when the little binkie thing was put into her mouth.

"There are things about this that make me think the woman was supposed to live. She wasn't buckled in, nor did there seem to be much in the way of drugs in her system."

Just as Venetia was going to say more, the woman woke up and started screaming. Nothing she was saying, however, was helpful in getting to the bottom of what had happened here today.

"My babies. My little babies. They're dead." Venetia told her that they weren't, actually. The look of shock was there and gone so quickly that had he not been looking at her, he would have missed it. "They're all right? When we went into the water, I thought we were all dead."

"No. Just the man there." She looked in the direction that Venetia pointed. "He didn't drown, either. I think he was murdered before going into the water."

"I don't know what you're talking about." She looked around. "Where is Wendy? She was in the backseat as well."

Looking along the shoreline, he saw Hale, Venetia's faerie, and Noodle, his faerie, laying a child on the ground. When he started for them, Noodle told him to stay away, then came to stand on his shoulder so she could speak to him.

"The child is fine, your lordship. She is afeared of her mother. Wendy, her name is, said her mother shot her daddy. She thought her asleep, as the others were. The little tyke said she pretended to fall asleep with the others so she could save them. But she hit her head and must have fainted before she could act." He asked if she could be taken to the house to be kept safe. "Yes. I'll take her myself. Also, you should know that the babe has been drugged before. The mother isn't a nice person."

"I'd say you were right." He asked if they had a name other than Wendy. Noodle told him all he knew was the child's first name. "My family is coming here now. Go to my mom and tell her what you told me. Then if you could have Daniel come here in the cruiser, we'll get this straightened out quickly."

The children were still upset, and the boy—his name was Sammy, it turned out—was sick. Twice now, he'd thrown up, and his mother ignored him for the most part. Looking at Venetia when she coughed, he watched as she put her finger to her lips and pointed at the woman. She was talking to herself, thinking that neither of them could hear her.

"What the fuck? What the glorious fuck? You couldn't even make sure you weren't found, could you, Samuel?" Leslie watched as she kicked the dead man. "I was going to be saved while you and the brats were dead. Mother fuck, I hate you more now than I did when you were living."

"Hello, son." He turned and hugged his mom while she fussed over the children. Handing each of them a bottle of juice, she changed out the one for the baby to a bottle of milk. "There you go. You just drink that down, and you'll feel so much better." Mom picked up the baby and looked at Leslie. "Daniel is on his way. Noodle is getting things ready at the house for our guests. The dray horses are being brought in to pull the car to the driveway so it can be taken away as well. Are you all right, Venetia?"

"Yes. Just peachy." There was a tone there that made him think she was far from peachy. But she did smile at Mom. "I'm assuming you've been privy to the things going on around here?"

"Yes. Hanna has been keeping us all updated." Mom winked at him before speaking to the other woman. "This is Mrs. Rebecca Canavan. Her husband was Samuel. The two children here are Sammy and Bethy."

"Where is Wendy? When you were saving the rest of us, where is Wendy?" Mom told Rebecca she was safe at her home. "Your home? Why? How did she get there? She was in the car with us when my husband decided to take a leap into the river."

"I don't think so." Hanna hugged first Venetia then him as she continued. Rebecca asked her what that was supposed to mean. "Samuel was dead a full hour before you put him in the car. The children had been drugged about the time you decided you didn't want them around you anymore either. You'll not lie to anyone again, Rebecca. By the way, your lover has been taken into custody. He is singing to anyone that is willing to listen about how you had the perfect plan. You should have made sure you really had drugged the children before you assumed they were unable to listen to your plans."

"What did that brat say?" She seemed to realize what she'd said and smiled. "I'm a little stressed about all this. What did Wendy have to say about anything going on? Just so you know, I've had disciplinary trouble with her for the last few years."

"Yes, you have. But only because you didn't like her telling Samuel there what you were up to. Why don't you tell us how you worked the plan out, Rebecca? I'm sure now that the police are here, you'd like to get it off your chest." Rebecca bit her lips so hard they were bleeding profusely. "Tell us. Now."

"I hate them all. All of them were sucking

the life right out of me. I wanted to get the insurance money so I could go off and reinvent myself." Mom asked about Samuel. "Samuel? Christ, if there was a more stupid father and lackluster person in the world, I'd never want to meet them. He would do anything for me but have his body thrown from the car so he'd not be found until he was nothing more than fish food. The kids too. Christ, how did Wendy survive that shit? I'll tell you how. She has nine lives. If you knew how many times I tried to rid my body of her before she came squirting out, you'd give me the golden ring. Then, after she was born, all she did was try and find ways to make me look bad. I should have shot her too. All of them."

Sammy got up and came to sit on Leslie's lap. Mom was feeding the baby still, and Venetia stood nearby. Rebecca was unhinged. Not only that, he was sure this wasn't her first attempt at getting rid of her family. She kept talking about how she would try again and that she'd win next time. Win what, he didn't even want to hazard a guess about. Daniel kept telling Rebecca that he was recording everything she said.

The horses arrived just as a couple of Feds walked onto the scene. They were still in town for the things that had been found on the Mission property. Once she was taken into custody, kicking and screaming about how it was Samuel's fault they were all alive, Mom handed him the baby.

Hooking up the car to the horses didn't take any time at all, and they were on their way in a few minutes. When they arrived at the house, he handed the baby over to Venetia so he could talk to Daniel first, as he had been first on the scene. Venetia would too, but he wasn't going to mess this up for the kids. Their mother was going to prison, hopefully for a very long time.

Leslie had been a police officer before. He, along with his brothers, had been a lot of different things. Being a cop was something he didn't like at all, not even on the best days. Daniel seemed to be having a better time than he'd been having before. Having had his Parkinson's taken care of certainly made him more relaxed about everything, he thought.

Rebecca was taken away once she was able to tell her story again. It seemed like a slam dunk, but he knew better than to count on that. Stranger things had happened before. As he held the baby while Venetia told her side of what happened, Wendy came to sit next to him and her sister.

"She's so little, and Mom wanted her dead." Leslie told her he was sorry for that. "Me too. I tried hard to make sure she was no trouble, but I couldn't take her to school with me. She would give her drugs while I was gone. I'm so sorry about that."

"You did everything you could, honey. Including telling the police what you'd seen at the time of your father's death." She nodded as she held onto Bethy's hand. "My brother, the doctor, Marley, said all of you are in good shape but need to eat better. I don't think you'll have that trouble for very long. My mom and my brothers will keep you here until someone can be notified to come and get you. Do you have any aunts or uncles that might want to take care of you guys?"

"Nobody is left. Mom had a brother, but he killed himself a few years ago." She looked up at him with shock on her face. "Do you think she killed him too? I'd not put it past her anymore. She killed the lady that came to dust the house too. The police officer wants me to go and show him where the bodies are."

"Bodies?" She nodded and watched her sister fall asleep. "You can stay with us for as long as you need to, Wendy. We'll never let anything happen to you. I swear it."

"Thank you, Mr. Leslie."

Putting Bethy on the blanket on the floor, he went to find his mom. He knew where she'd be. The kitchen was a place she'd go when she had something to work out. He only hoped she wasn't trying to make bread again. It wouldn't be fit to eat if she was.

~*~

Venetia watched Morgan as she stirred the chips into the cookie batter. They'd not be chips for long, more like shavings if she kept at it the way she was. Taking the bowl and the spoon from her, she told her to have a seat, and she'd take care of the cookies. Venetia was just putting the first batch of cookies in the oven when Leslie came into the room.

"We'll need you to go into town and find something for the kids to wear. Also, bottles. I have plenty of milk from the cows this morning but no bottles." Venetia said she and Leslie would go after the cookies were done. Then she winked at Leslie when he whispered, asking about his mom. "Thank you. And I'm doing just fine, Leslie. Don't be rude. We'll need some cloth diapers too. I'm not even sure they make them anymore."

"I think so, but I'd not use them either. They're full of chemicals to make them not stain as much. I can take care of that and the bottles for you." Morgan nodded and seemed to be lost in thought. Venetia looked at Leslie when he took a hot cookie from the sheet pan. "Hale told me that he was my faerie. Noodle also introduced herself to me." He said he was sorry about that. He'd meant to do it today. "No reason to be. It's not like we've had a normal day so far. Anyway, Noodle and Hale are going to fashion a baby bed for Bethy. If you've no problem with them being with us, I'd like to make sure the kids have a place to sleep that they can call their own."

"Wendy and I were just talking about that. I'd very much like it if they would be our children if you would like that. I also should have told you I have a place for us to live." She asked him where it was. "Here. The seven of us, including Mom, have lived here our whole life, and with the magic we were gifted, we were able to take our rooms and make them into something much larger than it appears from the hallway. You and I have four bedrooms, living, dining, and a few other rooms in the one we have. Also, we can change it around any way you wish, but I think we can be comfortable living here. If not, then we'll think of something else."

"No. I think I'd like to be right here. This is the heart of this family, and I like that we can live here and be separate from the rest when we want to. All right. I'll make sure things are set up how the kids will want them. If, as you said, they need or want something different, then we can work on that. Do you know if there is anyone else we can contact?" He told her what Wendy had said to him. "I can look into that, but I'd have to be with the body. I'm to understand that Hanna can do that sort of thing. Find lifelines to people with only their name." Leslie laughed and said she could do amazing things. "Yes, well, I've picked up a couple more things too since coming here. I can—"

"The children. They're going to need someplace to live. I can make sure they're well fed, but as far as raising them, I'm not sure how good I'd be any more at being a motherly type. I'm a great deal older than I used to be. I wouldn't know the first thing about new rules and such." They all laughed about that. Venetia didn't tell Morgan when she spoke up that they'd already discussed that very thing. Instead, Leslie told his mom what he was thinking, and she nodded at him. "They'll be safe here. Also, they'll get some good food in their bellies. I'm thinking they've not had much in the way of home cooked anything for a while, if ever."

"Mom, are you all right?" Morgan stared at Leslie when he asked her. "You seem to be thinking very hard about something. Tell us so we can help you."

"She was willing to kill her own children." Venetia had an idea that was what was bothering the other woman. Leslie hugged his mom as she sobbed out her hurt at what had been done to the children. "I can't stand the fact that she isn't going to die the same way she hoped her children would have. People, humans, aren't even nice to their own offspring. Are they, Leslie?"

"Mom, I was going to talk to Venetia later about this, but I'd like to adopt the children. All three of them." Venetia said that was what she was hoping to do as well. "Then it's settled. You'll have three more grandchildren to spoil rotten and fatten up as much as you wish. If we can convince the courts to allow us to have them."

"They'd better if they don't want me to come down on their asses." Morgan perked up after that. She even smiled when she took one of the cookies off the cooling rack. "Let me make a few phone calls on your behalf. I think they'll be good for all of us around here too. What with Hanna and Piper having babies, it'll be like we've finally got something to celebrate at the holidays. Thank you both for this."

Morgan left them, and Venetia finished up the cookies. She noticed that Leslie only ate them when they were hot out of the oven, but he didn't eat all that many either. Thinking of being a mom to three kids, she wondered what else was going to be in store for the two of them when Leslie spoke, interrupting her thoughts.

"We should get married. I know this is fast, but I think we'll stand a better chance of getting the children if we're a married couple." She told him that was fine by her. "Whether you want a large or small wedding, it can be easy enough to arrange. However, we have people that can file that we're already married now so that when Mom makes her calls, the paperwork will be finalized."

"I'll talk to my parents, but go ahead and have everything filed. Also, so you're aware, I'm in love with you." He stood up so quickly that she backed away from him. "Did I say something wrong?"

"Never, when you tell me you love me. I

love you as well." He moved toward her slowly. "I'd like to kiss you right now. I'd like to take you upstairs and make you mine, but I know there are things going on that are going to need our attention right now."

She kissed him anyway. Knowing that at any moment anyone could walk in on them, she pulled away when he tried to lift her up to the counter. It took her fuzzy mind a few seconds to realize that the timer was going off for the next batch of cookies. Pushing him to the side, she scolded him for being in her way. All he did was laugh.

"I'll be back later. My room is the one at the top of the stairs on the left. It has a yellow door." She turned and looked at him, asking if he wanted her to wait on him. "No reason for that. You make notes of whatever you think we'll need, as well as the kids. Hale will be with you if you need something right away. Barring that, you can have him bring in the faeries and take care of most anything you wish. Also, just to give you a heads up, they take everything you say literally. Like, if you tell them you want the room painted, you must tell them the walls. Otherwise, they'll have the entire room the same color. Same with the kitchen appliances. I know we're going to need a larger refrigerator, but tell them you want one that'll fit a certain space. For some reason, they think the bigger things are, the better you're going to like it. Trust me on this one. We'll have a walk-in refrigerator if you're not specific with them."

She thought he was kidding her, and after he left, she put the cookies that were cooled enough in a tin she'd found. Her sister joined her as she was pulling things out of the pantry to make some other kinds of cookies for the kids to snack on.

"Did you know they send their wheat out to be milled, and that's why they have flour?" She told Zippy she'd not seen that as yet. "They do everything right here. When Bailey told me that, I thought he was joking. They don't even own a car or truck but use horses to do the plowing and moving of the foodstuffs. I've not had an opportunity to talk to you much since we arrived. How are you, Veni?"

Smiling at the shortened version of her name, she answered her. "I'm doing well now that I have my memories back. Some I wish I'd never had, but they're all there. I'm a good deal stronger as a witch than I was before. Do you suppose it has to do with being here?" Zippy told her that was something she was working out too. She was mixing the batch of coconut cookies when Zippy asked her if she hated her. "Why on earth would you think I hate you?"

"I should have gone back for you. I tried to find what happened to you, but you were so small when you were taken that your magic hadn't been acquired by you yet. I could have found you easier if I had had some kind of tag to look for. I'm so sorry." Veni held her sister as she cried, telling her over and over that it was all right. She'd had enough to deal with in taking care of their parents. "Did the other family treat you well? That's all I've been thinking about since I heard you'd been found."

"They were nice to me. I knew from an early age I wasn't theirs. I didn't know the entire story, but most of it. I thought my parents were dead. I don't know that they knew about you at all. It was never something that came up." She went back to making the batter for the cookies while her sister composed herself. "I was working for the FBI about Henderson and Applegate. I was getting very close to having all the information needed to bring them in when they caught me one night looking in files that I had no access to during working hours. Luckily I was able to send off what I had before I was tossed from the car."

"I'd like to be a part of making them pay for what they did to you. To all of us." Veni told her she'd have to stand in line. So would her new brothers. Zippy smiled then. "It's strange, isn't it? That both of us are mated to brothers. Our children will be double cousins or something. Don't you think?"

Wendy came into the room then with Bethy in her arms. Zippy took her from the older child and put her in the highchair she was sure wasn't there before. As soon as Bethy was strapped in, Wendy asked if they could have a snack. Since she'd baked the kids the cookies for after dinner, she cut them both up an apple — smushed up for Bethy and sliced for Wendy — then after cutting grapes into smaller pieces for the baby again, Veni put some grapes on the plate, and gave both the little girls some juice.

"When we lived at home with Momma, she wouldn't let us have any juice. She said it was for mixing whiskey in and not for brats." Veni looked at her sister when she started to speak. Shaking her head just enough, Zippy asked Wendy how often she would be putting juice and whiskey together. "Every day. She'd give a bottle of it to Bethy, too, when she was fussy. That seemed to be all the time. But she'd pinch her too."

"Your mother would pinch the baby?" Morgan came in and sat down at the table with the girls and shared the grapes she was cutting in half for Bethy. "I'm assuming she did similar things to you and your brother?"

"Yes. Mostly it was to lock us in the room. We called it that because that's all it was. No lights or rugs. There wasn't even a window we could open. Just a pot in the corner for us to do our business in." Wendy handed Bethy a sippy cup that Morgan had. Things were popping up all over the place for the children, Venetia thought with a laugh. "I saved all the bottles she gave us to drink from too. I didn't ever drink enough to go to sleep, as Bethy and Sammy did. Someone had to watch them. So the night we were put in the car, I was wide awake, and I got out before the car flipped over. I couldn't save them then. I got tangled up in some branches that hung me in the water for a long time. Until Noodle came to rescue me."

After finding out where Wendy had hidden the half-empty bottles of water, Veni, a nickname that was growing on her, told Leslie where she was going. He told her he'd meet her there with the police and for her to be careful.

I'm going to kill her is what I'm going to do. He asked her to wait on that. *I'll give it my best shot. But she drugged these children — they're very lucky to be alive, I'm thinking, after the way they were treated. Damn it, Leslie, I'm pissed.*

So am I, honey. I'll meet you at the house. Be careful. And bring Zippy with you. I think between the two of you, we'll have no trouble finding all the little things around the house that were used against our kids. She liked the sound of that and told him so. *I like it too. I love you, Venetia. So be careful.*

She decided to tell him her new nickname later. Right now, she needed to put her focus on the task at hand and look for enough evidence to put Rebecca Canavan behind bars forever.

Chapter 2

Leslie had to go outside. The house and the smell were almost too much for him to be around. His cat was also unhappy with the things that had been left undone, things left out to rot so the maggots could get to it. He gagged twice before he could calm himself enough to be able to go back into the house.

"The health department and child welfare are all over this place. It seems the Canavan's power was turned off several weeks ago, and there isn't any running water that they can find. How the hell could you raise kids in this place?" Leslie told Zippy he had no idea why anyone would live like this. "She left things out so the place wouldn't be inhabitable once she was found alive. And that was her plan too. I'm sure you've figured that out."

"The boyfriend — Brian, I think his name is — told us everything he could. Apparently, he was forced into this relationship with Rebecca when he was seventeen. Now that he's twenty, the kid just wants to move away and start a new life. Mom is going to help him with that. He had no idea Rebecca was married, nor that she had three kids." Zippy looked around the yard. "The city is going to have the place torn down. Once they do that, the faeries will come in and plant the entire place with flowers. That'll leave the ground in better shape than it is now."

"Will you buy it too?" He said that as a family, they'd decide on it. "I'd like to purchase it if you don't mind. I have it in my head to put in a Wicca shop. Not just things a witch might need, but also things like dried herbs. I have a very nice line of lotions and such that I'd like to make on a grander scale." She looked at him. "I'm going to need something to do to keep me busy. Do you think your brother will mind if I work?"

"I don't see where he'd have any thoughts at all of keeping you from doing anything you wish. We're not the type of men that most are, especially humans. Our mother died when we were one. Then Morgan raised us with no more knowledge of men or shifters than most preschoolers have. The one thing she made sure we understood was that not only is a woman's body her own but that she has a brain and opinions as well."

"Your mother did a great job if she has you all thinking like that." Zippy turned and looked at him before speaking again. "I'm assuming it makes no difference to any of you that we're witches either, does it?"

"No. So long as you're happy, we are too." He waited for her to say more, but when she didn't, he spoke again. "What's going on, Zippy? Has someone said something to you? I hope that's not it."

"No. No one has said anything to me other than that I'm a very lucky woman." She turned away again. "I don't know my sister. Not at all. I hate that too. It's like we're strangers to each other, and I don't know how to make it any different."

"You have a lifetime of memories you can make with her now, Zippy. More than that, you can start fresh if you wish. Veni told me that you and her are going to do some work together around town. I think that's wonderful. And the shop? Well, I'm excited to see what you have going with that. The other women here, all of them, I think they will learn a great deal from the two of you." She asked him what he meant by that. "You can show them that distance and absence don't matter. Love is the most important thing you can have and share. Also, I think now that you're here and with the fact you are used to using magic, you could help the others with theirs. That would go a long way in making a tighter bond between you and the others."

"I don't have any friends. I mean, there are a couple of people I can talk to, but no friends I'd call on if I needed something. Your mom is terrific. So are the others. Hanna, frankly, scares the shit out of me in the things she can do, but she'd not nasty about it." Zippy laughed. "It's like she has this chip on her shoulder for everyone but us to see. And I think she's in awe of your mom too. It's wonderful having all of them around all the time." He told her that was just the way it should be with family. "I suppose it is. It's been only myself and my parents for so long that I'm actually looking forward to being around people all the time. That's why I think this shop will be good for me. A place to meet others like me or to just talk to someone about something other than the aches and pains of my parents. Don't get me wrong, I'm thrilled to have them around. But it's nice being around people my age again."

"Good. Then we've done a good thing for all of us."

They both moved out of the way when the police came out of the house. They'd been taking turns going in and letting the others have a breather. He nearly groaned when he saw Mom coming toward them. She had not only Sammy but Wendy as well.

"Wendy has some things she wants to tell them while they're here." He held Sammy's hand while he buried his face in Leslie's pants. Mom spoke to him from their link as she asked Daniel to come out and talk to Wendy about some things. *I think he's a little upset that he came now. I did ask him, and he wanted to come. But getting here, he's not doing so well. Take him to get some ice cream or something, Leslie. He could use it.*

"Hey, buddy. You want to go to the store with me? I have to get a few things for Veni. We're having supper at our place tonight." He hoped they were. Leslie led the little boy to the store, and they got a cart. It occurred to him that Sammy had never been in a grocery store before.

The way he was looking around made him think the kid was more sheltered than he'd thought. "My mom never wanted us to eat processed foods when we were little. But I have to tell you, I sneak in a box of cereal once in a while. Makes me appreciate the things we have on the farm. Did you know we even make our own cheese and whipped cream? Best there is."

"My mom said that buying dinners already cooked was the only way people with money did it. I never liked the stuff she'd bring us." He was looking in the bins of fruit that Leslie was looking at. "Those don't look like the apples you have at your house, Mr. Leslie. Those look like they're sick. Why is that?"

"More than likely they are. There will be chemicals on them that farmers put on the trees to keep the bugs away. Mom won't use them. That's why we're all so healthy." Sammy seemed to be satisfied with that answer. He picked up and put back peaches and grapes before he found something he seemed to like. "What do you have there?"

Hummus? The only other person that liked hummus as much as he did was Shiloh. And he'd eat all Mom made in one sitting if he could. He asked Sammy if he'd ever had it before.

"No. But it looks like hums. So it has to be good, right?" Laughing, he put it in the cart, hoping his mom would forgive him for this one purchase. "What the heck is that?"

It took him a few minutes to figure out what he was looking at. Not that he didn't know what watermelon was, but he couldn't believe he hadn't had one before. While he knew there was plenty of the wonderful fruit at home, he decided he was going to buy this one, and they were going to eat it right out in the parking lot.

They ended up with only a few things in their cart before deciding they had better stuff at home. He told Veni what they were doing and what Wendy was doing with Mom. She had just put Bethy down for a nap and was going to go through their rooms. Leslie told her she could change anything she wanted.

The watermelon went over better than he could have hoped for. Not only did Sammy love it, but he liked it with salt on it as much as Leslie did. They were just finishing off the last slice when his mom came to find him. Wendy looked a little worse for wear, and Mom said she was taking her to buy some things for her room.

"She gave me a blanket she made for my bed, Mr. Leslie. It's the most beautiful thing I've ever seen. Grandma Morgan is going to show me how to use the loom, too, when all this is settled with the idiots." He asked her who the idiots might be. "My biological parents. Can I call you Dad? I had one, but he wasn't very helpful with Rebecca. That's what I'm going to call her from now on. I know more and more that she wasn't nice to any of us at all."

When Wendy sat down with her brother, Leslie looked at his mom. Her eyes were sparkling with unshed tears, and he held her while he got ahold of his own emotions. Dad. She wanted to call him Dad.

"Well, Grandma Morgan, what's your plans for the rest of the evening? Want to come up to our place and have a few slices of pizza? That's what Veni is going to make for us." She nodded, and he hugged her tighter. "Mom, if you cry right now, you and I both are going to be a sloppy mess, and that will do none of us any good. All right?"

"Yes. All right." She looked up at him. "I don't know when I've been happier, Leslie. Grandchildren around. My boys with mates. I so wish Golden Eyes, your biological mother, could see you all now. She'd be in heaven right about now."

"I have a feeling she's watching us all the time for a good laugh." He told her about the watermelon. "I couldn't help but to buy it for him. He'd never seen one, much less had a treat of eating one out in the open. Sammy can spit seeds further than you can, I'm betting."

Mom took Wendy to the store, but as soon as they walked into the place, they were coming right out. He waited to find out if someone had said something when he realized they were both laughing. Almost too hard for him to understand.

"She can dress herself." Well, he thought, he certainly hoped so. She was twelve. Then it occurred to him what she meant. "She found this pretty little shirt that I was going to have her try on when she was suddenly wearing it. I had her change back before someone thought we were stealing it, but oh, Leslie, you should have heard her squeal."

"I was shocked, that's all." Wendy laughed again. "I'm going to look at magazines to see what sort of things I can wear. We never had new stuff when we went to school, but this will be so much fun for us."

Wendy showed Sammy how he could change his clothing too. All he could think about was how disappointing it was going to be for them to not have to go school shopping. Veni was actually talking about doing that today. Going by the house again, Sammy and Wendy stayed with his mom. He didn't blame them for not wanting to go in. Leslie sort of wished he didn't have to either.

"We've found some money stashed around the house. A great deal of it, as a matter of fact. Not sure what she had it earmarked for, but you can bet we'll make sure the kids get it." Leslie told Daniel to use it for the mister's funeral. "That's better. I'm guessing they won't need it so long as you have them. By the way, I heard the auction for the gems is going to be the day after tomorrow. The only reason I know about it is because your mom had me take them to the auction house as security. I'm going to be on duty to be around for the show too."

"I'm sure they could always use a good man to help out. I'm glad it's going to be you." He was too. After his close brush with death, the other man had taken on an entirely new outlook on life, especially when it came to his own family. "Will you make sure the funeral is paid for out of the money? If there is any leftover, we'll set it aside for the woman to use for her defense. Not that she deserves a good attorney, but that will be better than telling the kids there was money there all along for them to use."

"I can do that. It would be my pleasure. I heard that Hanna went to make arrangements for Mr. Canavan already, so this will go a long way in paying for it. Thank you for that." He nodded his answer. "There are some other things around here that need to be taken care of, the house not included. We've found where Samuel worked. Now we're going to notify them of his death and see if there were any death benefits from there. I'll let you know."

That made him remember that the will needed to be read for Blanche and her sister. That was what had brought all the women here, to see what the old biddies had left for their children. Whatever it was, he was happy she'd brought the family together. Even if she didn't have a thing to do with him and his brothers being happy.

When he'd answered all he could with the FBI and the police, he made his way to where the kids were. As he was checking to make sure they had everything they needed, it occurred to him that he was going to be a dad soon. Almost as soon as he thought of that, he had to hold onto the lamp post nearby so that he didn't fall over. A dad? Christ, who would have thought it.

As they made their way home, he pointed out some of the things going on around town. Also, some of the upcoming events they might enjoy. Leslie was looking forward to the Fourth celebrations. The entire town would gather together, and they'd roast a hog and a cow for the meat. The other families would bring covered dishes. Then as the sun went down, they'd set off fireworks that rivaled even the biggest of towns.

Veni was still on the upper floor, so he took the other two up with him. He found her in the kitchen with Noodle and Hale, making a list of things she'd like to have done to the house. As they passed the living room, he noticed that his old furniture was gone and the room had been painted, but he wasn't upset. In fact, he'd been thinking of changing it for some time now.

"We're having pizza tonight." Veni had thought the kids would enjoy making their own, but she didn't mention that to them. Leslie wondered if they'd ever had a hot pizza and decided not to ask. Bethy was up and crawling around on the floor, so he picked her up and took her with him to the dining room.

Veni had put her stamp on this room as well. The room was brighter. It took him a few seconds to realize she'd not only had the room painted, but she'd enlarged it as well. There were plates in the cabinets that he hadn't seen in decades, and he was glad now that he'd kept them. Not that he knew where they came from, but they were being used, and that was great.

Leslie was headed to the kitchen again when he heard Veni telling Wendy and Sammy about their faeries.

"They will be with you forever. And not that I think you'll be any trouble, but they'll also be there to guide you to the right decisions." Setting Bethy in the highchair, he told them they'd also have magic. "Yes. A thing you'll have to keep hidden away because it'll get you into trouble if someone sees you using it."

"You mean they'll take us to make us use it for evil." Veni just managed to stop herself from laughing when she told Sammy that was right. "I've been watching television since we got here. They sure do mess up things like magic and faeries. They have them all looking like they're all sparkly all the time when they're really only sparkly when they have their wings out. Then they're bea-u-ti-ful."

He said that in four drawn out syllables, which to Leslie's way of thinking made it all the more important of a word for the young man.

Cutting grapes in half for Bethy, he sort of half listened to the things going on around the table. Getting up to steam some carrots and other fresh vegetables for the baby, he turned to look at Wendy when she spoke.

"I'm sorry. What did you say?" She dropped her head like she thought she was in trouble. "I'm not upset. I'm sorry if that's what you thought. But did you just tell me that you got to see Mr. Weeds? He's very special to the grounds here and is rarely seen by anyone he's not introduced to."

"He told me that." Wendy looked at him. "Mr. Weeds was asking me to find him some parts he could use for his watering system. We worked on it for most of yesterday until he was ready for a nap. He said the only way to think clearly is to be rested and full. But they both don't last for long, so eat food when you find it. I like him."

"I do too. And I have parts for him in my office. After dinner, we'll get them, and you can take them to him tomorrow. In the meantime, I wanted to tell you how proud I am of you being around creatures you don't know, but you're willing to help them. That's what makes this place run so well." Wendy was proud of herself then. Leslie made sure that Bethy's food was cooled off and gave it to her. "I was told yesterday by Grandma Morgan that there is a larger gathering of magical creatures today. If you'd like to go with her, she wanted me to warn you that you have to be very still and quiet unless you can contribute to what's going on. Some of the people there are very tiny and can get hurt if there is a lot of running around. Also, magical creatures can hear better than humans, so shouting can harm them."

Wendy had already been asked to go by Mom, but she did have to ask them. Sammy, age nine, promised to be on his best behavior, and Leslie held him to the promise. He wasn't a bad kid at all, but he did get excited when something new was put before him. However, Leslie also knew that if anyone could manage him, it would be Mom. Bethy, at seven months, would stay at home with Hanna.

~*~

Rebecca had her defense all figured out. Blaming it all on Samuel would work because he couldn't defend himself anymore. Him being dead was going to work in her favor anyway, even though he'd fucked up everything else she'd had planned out.

He would have been found months from now if she'd had everything perfect. His bloated body would no longer show signs of being shot. There would be very little left of him after the fishes got their tasty meal off his body.

Then there were the kids. She'd gone to a great deal of trouble and expense to have them alive right now. When each of them had been popped out, she made sure she took out a large insurance policy on them so that in the hopeful event of them dying, she'd have something to use for all the shit she'd had to endure to bring them into the world. Even that had been a total fuck up. But at least she didn't have to look at them anymore. For now, anyway.

Rebecca hadn't known that Wendy wasn't taking the drugs she'd made up for the kids. She should have. The kid was too smart for her own good sometimes. The fact that she wasn't in the car should have been the first thing that alerted her. The second thing was, she had been taken to someone's home. That alone made her think that not only wasn't she drugged, but she was awake and talking rather than in the morgue where she should have been.

Also, Wendy could never be depended on to keep her mouth shut. Like them being without power. She'd told the school the day before they went on their little river trip, and that was going to suck for her if anyone went by their home.

Why was there a need for something like electricity when all the kids did was come home from school, which was lit up like a Christmas tree, to have more lights when they got home? Didn't make the least bit of sense to her. Yes, she did suppose it made it difficult for her to have a clean glass when she needed it. But that was what the hose was for.

She'd been stealing water from her neighbors since she'd been out on her own. Not just water, but anything she could take without having to pay for it. Not having power had made it so she'd been able to stash away hundreds of thousands of dollars for run money. Rebecca wondered if anyone had bothered to take the brats to the house yet. They'd better not be bothering her things. That's all she had to say about that.

There were so many things about her that even her first husband hadn't known. He'd been a putz. Not only had he not allowed her to skip out on things like paying the bills, but he'd kept tight reins on the money too. He had it, and she wasn't going to get it, was his favorite thing to say to her when she asked for some extra.

However, Harry had loved his son. Richard had been a surprise to her. Just like the other three kids, she couldn't rid him from her body no matter what she tried. When he was born, all nine pounds of him, she thought for sure that would be the end of her. But she healed and came to resent Richard from the moment someone put him into her arms.

Killing him had been easier than any other death she'd done. Just put him in the bathtub and walk away. It wasn't until years later that her brother Toby had figured out what she'd done—or at least, that was when he brought it up, telling her not to drown the kids she had now. Three weeks later, Toby was dead, and no one was the wiser of it being her that murdered him.

Smiling at the memories, she thought of killing the housekeeper because she got pissy about the no water thing. The man who lived across the street had taken a nasty tumble down his front steps last winter. There were others, at least a dozen, that she was responsible for killing, including her first husband and parents. Rebecca didn't like killing, not really, but she didn't like having loose ends. It was why she had avoided any jail or prison time after all this time.

However, she wasn't entirely sure why she was in jail now. She'd not been driving the car that went into the river. There wasn't any way that anyone could prove she'd drugged her children. Again, that was something that was going to be blamed on Samuel, not her. Yes, they were aware that he'd been shot, but he'd been depressed of late due to money issues, and he'd shot himself before trying to kill off her entire family. Damn it to all fuck and back, Samuel had become more trouble than it had been worth to give him the three brats.

"Mrs. Canavan? There is someone here to see you. Also, you've not signed off on the paperwork for your husband's body to be taken care of. That seems to be a habit of yours." She didn't care for her jailer, but then, they were all assholes. "You have a hearing tomorrow afternoon too."

"I want him cremated. Like I've told you several times now. Also, there isn't to be any kind of funeral for him. No one would want to go see a man who tried to kill his entire family." She was starting now on her story so it would be perfected by the time she was brought before a judge. "Why do I have to see a judge? For that matter, no one has told me why I'm in here in the first place. Where are the bra—my children? Is someone taking care of them?"

"A damn better job of it than you ever did." Rebecca knew who the woman was that was seated across from her, but not the others. She and Hanna Golden didn't hang out together because Hanna had more money than sense. Rebecca hated—with a passion—rich people. "Have a seat. Then we'll go over some of the things you should expect for tomorrow. This gentleman, to my right, is the attorney standing in for your children. The man to his right is Mr. Pettiford, who is standing in for the family of Harold and Richard Lipscomb. The other—"

"What are you talking about? I don't know these people." Hanna told her that was why she was introducing them to her. "What I mean is, why are people here for my first husband and son? Don't you think I've suffered enough this week?"

Forcing herself to cry wasn't going to be possible, so Rebecca faked it the best she could. When she glanced around the room, she knew she wasn't fooling anyone. Putting the tissue she'd grabbed on the table, Rebecca glared at the younger woman as she continued to tell her that the FBI was there, as well as child welfare.

"Before you ask me why I'm here, I'll tell you. I'm here as a moderator. I'm really good at it, and the groups represented here asked me to sit in with them, so if there was any trouble, I could knock the shit out of you and go again." The man at her right cleared his throat. "Okay, I'm not supposed to hit you, but I'm telling you right now, I will if you give any of them any shit. Do you understand these things as they've been told to you?"

"No. I don't understand any of this. Why is child welfare here?" The woman that was there for that told her. "What do you mean, child endangerment? I had nothing to do with my kids being in that car. It was all Samuel. He was the bad guy in this."

"Was he? Really? Because I have it on good authority that not only did you kill your husband, Mrs. Canavan, but you also drugged your children prior to the car going down the embankment and into the river." She looked at the picture that was put in front of her. It was blurry at first, but the woman told her what she was looking at, and it started to make sense to her. "You're standing right there in your own yard with a gun pointed at the driver of the car.

If you look hard enough, you can also see that it's your husband."

Wow. That was all she could think about was *wow*. It was as crisp and clear as if the woman talking had been standing right next to her with the camera. The next picture was of her carrying the children out to the car and putting them in the back. Christ, who the hell had been taking these pictures?

"They're stills from a house camera behind your home."

Okay, she supposed that was something she'd have to remember for next time. As the woman droned on, Rebecca couldn't believe the amount of information they had on her over this one murder.

Then the man from the FBI began to speak. "We're also looking into the deaths of your first husband and son. There are too many similarities to other deaths that happened while you were on watch." She asked him who else did he think she killed other than drowning her son. Everyone just sat there looking at her. "Did you just admit to drowning your son, your five week old son, Ms. Canavan?"

"I don't know what you're talking about." For the next several hours, she repeated over and over how she didn't know what they were talking about. Each time they brought up some new detail, like her brother Toby's supposed suicide, she'd repeat it. Then they mentioned the money they'd found. "What do you mean snooping through my things? I will own your asses if you think I'm—"

"Why do people say that you think? Own our asses, I mean." Rebecca looked at Hanna. "You really think it's a good thing to own someone else's ass? What would you do with it? I mean, it's not like it would make a good conversation piece in your home. Although I have been in yours, and I'm thinking it might be an improvement. But seriously—"

"What the fuck are you talking about?" Hanna told her never mind. "I want my money brought to me here. That way, I can make sure none of you idiots can touch it. When I get out of here, I'm going to need it."

"You're not getting out." She looked at the FBI guy when he spoke. As he was leaning back in his chair, he smiled. "We have you on so many counts—theft of welfare money, theft, insurance fraud, murder of at least six people, and still counting. Attempted murder of three minors. Christ, woman, you'll be lucky if you ever see the light of day again after you leave here. I do have an offer for you. You plead guilty to all of the charges, and I'll make sure you get twenty minutes daily outside. Alone, of course."

"I want a lawyer." Each of them stood up like they'd been put on springs. The only one left after they were gone was Hanna. "I don't want to talk to you either. You'll twist things around until I might admit to killing you. Though I do think that has merit."

"You just threatened an agent of the FBI, Rebecca. I put in my notice, you see, to quit my job with them, but they think I can do a great deal of work for them, sort of behind the scenes, so to speak." Rebecca hated this woman and told her so. "I don't care what your feelings are about me, Becky dear. But I will point out, not once have you asked after the health of your children. How they're doing. I would have wondered had they been mine. I know you had it in your head to go with the defense of it all being on Samuel, but that doesn't fly when you haven't cared for them any more than you did him." Hanna stood up. "One more thing I want to let you know about, then I won't bother you again. You should have taken better care to gather up the bottles of tainted water you gave the kids. Also, the heroin you used was still lying about in your house, with your fingerprints all over it."

It wasn't until she was back in her cell that she realized how right Hanna had been. She knew for a fact that there were several bottles on the kitchen table, along with the stuff she put into them, that were still full of the tainted water. There would be no one's fingerprints on them but hers, too. That was her fun, filling the bottles with heroin so she could watch the kids drink it down after a day without anything to drink. Fuckity fuck, she was going to fry.

Chapter 3

The auction was ready to begin in the morning. While it was going on, only two of them would be there. The rest of the family had decided to make a weekend of it and stay in New York. Leslie and Carroll were going to be the ones at the auction, and they were told in order to throw off suspicion of why they were there, to purchase or bid only on one of the pieces.

"Since the family rarely leaves your compound, people will be curious why you decided to come out for this one particular auction. I'm only trying to save you a great deal of privacy." They agreed with the man in charge of their auction and even decided on which piece they'd buy. "Very good, gentlemen. I think this will keep a great many people away from sniffing around for a clue as to who might have brought such a wonderful collection in. Did you read the story we've been putting out there?"

"Yes. I thought it was very clever of you to say it was from a private collector and that they've been collecting for years." The two of them looked at the collection they'd been digging up over the past weeks and found that there was a great deal more than they'd first thought. Of course, sending it in as they got it was why it hadn't occurred to them. "You said the arrowheads would go for a good deal more than you first thought. I don't think I heard why."

Leslie had meant to ask someone about that before they arrived and was glad now that Carroll had brought it up. He explained how the auction house had brought someone in to appraise them, and the age of the arrowheads was much older than they had thought. The value of them and their authentication would make people want them more.

Their attorney was there too. Usually, he or one of his brothers would make sure someone was on hand in the event something came up, as they had all been attorneys at one time or another. But as they were trying very hard not to draw any attention to themselves, this was a better way to go. With there being so much here that had been brought in by the family, Leslie was sure something was going to come up or go wrong.

"Have you heard anything about Henderson and Applegate?" Carroll said he'd not. "I have a couple of people watching them all the time. Well, faeries. But the two of them are plotting on how to make everything that has happened with the paperwork Veni found fall back on her plate. They seem to think anyone and everyone will believe she was the mastermind of the drugs and prostitution ring. Not that I don't think she could do it if she set her mind on it. But she is a great deal smarter about the law than I am. I might, after things settle down, open a practice with her. Nothing but the family and our charity work, but I think we could make some big headway into getting it right the first time with contracts and such."

"Mom was telling me that yesterday. How things aren't as easy as they used to be. A nod and a handshake were all she needed on things. Now, however, you have to have a contract for every little thing, and it had better have an iron-clad loophole for us to get out of too. It's a frightening world we've come into, I think."

They continued down the line of things that were marked with the catalog number they were going over for the auction house. Then Leslie thought of something. "Did Mom talk to you about this money we have coming from this? If there is any money from this auction?"

"No. I know she was upset about the will reading for Allison and her brother, as well as Meredith. There shouldn't be a charge for someone having a will read. I know that upset her. Also, the fact that they wouldn't turn over the check, the little that it was until they paid them for the reading. Sharks. I would have done it if there hadn't have been a conflict of interest with the families." He said he would have too. "What does she want to do with this money? I know you're going to get a portion of it for that repair shop—great idea on that. But what else is she thinking?"

"She wants to use some of the land on the other end of the property to put in teaching gardens. Some of the money we make here today will buy all the supplies and also put in a greenhouse. Mom said there isn't any point in going at this a little at a time, but to be fully on board so the next generation can learn. There won't be any chemicals used either. And the water will come from the natural spring in the back of the land." Carroll looked interested, for which he was glad. It was going to be entirely a family project. "It would be for high school freshmen and older, including college kids that want to go into green planting and growing."

"Then what happens when they drop out?" Leslie asked his brother if he was forever looking on the bad side of things. "No. I'm nervous about things, I guess. The land is ours, and we've all worked very hard on keeping people out. I'm worried that bringing people onto any part of our property will just open us up to shit we don't need."

"Mom thought of that too. She's going to make sure there is enough magic around the area that no one can move beyond where they're working. As for the dropouts, she said she'd make them pay back the time and effort that went into wherever they were in the gardening." Carroll said he liked that idea. "That's what I thought. But I also think she's been thinking about this for a long time. She had the entire thing laid out so it would work for everyone. Also, you didn't ask, but the kids will be able to use the work they do for college credits, as well as keep what they grow. They can sell it or share it, whatever they want, with their produce."

They were finishing up looking things over when Veni contacted him. She was calm, much too calm for his state of mind when she told him what was going on. He sat down as she spoke to him.

Don't freak out. He told her that wasn't a way to start a conversation. *No, but we have it managed, and that is all you need to think about. Your mom and Hanna were in town when there was a robbery at the bank. Why anyone would rob a bank on a Tuesday is beyond me. But it turns out it didn't matter the day anyway, as there was—* He asked her to get to the part where he needed to know it was all right. *I'm getting there. Just hold your horses. So, they were in the bank when this kid came in demanding that everyone lay on the floor. He was seventeen, and his parents were losing their home, along with everything else they owned. He figured that if he was caught, they'd turn him in for the reward money and save the day. Or if he managed to get the money, they'd be set. Okay, so Hanna touched the kid on the arm, and he fell to the floor. The gun wasn't even loaded. As your mom was calming the place the fuck down, I came into the bank too. Paperwork. Anyway, he confessed the entire reason why he was doing it. Your mom got pissed off—by the way, she's fucking scary when she* is calm and making a point. *She paid off the back taxes and bought the house from the bank, then handed the deed over to the young man. Hanna and I made sure no one pressed charges — well, we sort of took it out of their mind that anything happened. The money they were behind was only two dollars and fifty-six cents, Leslie. That's all. And they were foreclosing on the family for that. I tell you, I wish I had gotten to the banker before your mom did. He wouldn't be able to walk around. I'd have taken his dick off and made him sit there and eat it fucking raw.*

He laughed. It was a good story, and he was glad she'd let him know. *Where is the banker now?* She told him. *I wish I could have seen him being run out of town. You said his wife was leading the pack? Christ, that's the best thing I've heard all day. When are you guys coming up here?*

We're on our way to the airport now. Your mom is savvy, you know that, don't you? She made a single call, and we're using the airplane of someone she knows. He asked if Mom was doing all right. *She is. I think she's a little nervous, but right now, she's in the back seat with Bethy playing with her. I hope you were right in bringing the kids with us. I don't want them to be any trouble while this is going on. By the way, Wendy would like to go with you guys. I told her it was going to be boring, but she asked me to ask. But for us not to ask Carroll unless it's necessary. She and Sammy think he hates that they're in the household. He is sort of standoffish to them, don't you think? But, it'll be up to you on how you want to do this. She's excited to understand how things sell.*

I'll talk to Carroll about how he's treating them. However, I won't have an issue if she comes. I'd love to hear what she has to say about this. He told her what they were doing right now. *All of the gems are in a case with armed guards all around them. Every time we go to the next lot, we have to show our badges as well as wait for clearance. It's very well watched over.*

Good. I'd hate to get your mom to take care of them. She giggled. *Also, you'll be thrilled to know the bloodwork came back on all the kids. While there was some damage that isn't long-term with their developmental state of mind, the doctor said that with them being young and in a good home, they'll be just fine. Sammy has really attached himself to your mom. I've been watching him as he scoots himself closer to her a little at a time until she hugs him. I wonder if any of them had much in the way of love and hugs when they lived at their home.*

We'll make sure they're well-loved and hugged too. He looked at his brother when he sat down next to him. *I think we're finished here for the time being. We're to arrive early in the morning, then get a bidder number after having a look around. I'm nervous, to tell you the truth. I've never been to an auction before. I don't think Carroll has either, now that I think about it.*

You'll be fine. Both of you will. All right. I'm going to let you go. I don't know when we'll arrive, but we're set to head to the hotel after getting something to eat. I don't know what your mom will do when she has to eat processed food, but we'll see. She was laughing as she closed the connection.

Looking at Carroll, he asked him if he'd heard about the bank.

"I did. He's lucky we were here, or I would have tarred and feathered him on his way out. Hanna said she's going to find someone to run the bank in the meantime. I have all the faith in the world he'll be better than that jackass." Leslie agreed with him. "Hanna said to tell you that she's gotten a room for the kids. They'll have connecting doors for our room and yours. If you lock your end and tell them to come to us, we'll be able to give you an entire night of freedom."

"Is this your way of telling me I need to get laid?" Carroll laughed and said he was trying to be slick. "You weren't, just so you know. And thank you for that. I'll take you up on that."

"Good. Hanna has made arrangements to have champagne in the room, as well as a fully stocked fridge with snack foods. Consider it a wedding gift." He handed him the paperwork that said that he and Veni were married. "Also, I wanted to tell you that all the others are married as well. The paperwork was filed the same time yours was. I don't know if any of them will want a wedding, but they are wedded now."

"Thanks." Carroll was looking around the room. "What's eating you today? Or the last few days. You seem to be right on the edge of tearing a head off someone. Me included."

"I don't know what's wrong with me." Carroll finally looked at him. "I'm overwhelmed all the time. We still have to take care of a few things at home that need our attention instead of sitting around here with my thumb up my ass. The one that bothers me the most is how Veni was nearly left for dead alongside the road, and nothing is being done about that. Then there is the new information about the banker. A great many people have their money in there, and if they close it up for any reason, it's going to make it harder for people, including some of the older folks, to get their funds. I have a baby on the way, and I'm suddenly feeling the pressure of — what the hell was that for?"

The slap to his older brother's face wasn't that hard, but he could tell he was pissed about it. Before he allowed himself to answer, Leslie stood up and walked to the door. Telling Carroll to come with him, they were getting lunch, they left the building together before ending up at a nice local place. They were seated right away.

"Didn't I just tell you that Mom and your very own wife had things managed about the bank?" He nodded. "A baby on the way? Christ, Carroll, I have three children, and you don't hear me bitching about it. It's an amazing feeling having kids around. You'd see that too if you got your head out of your ass and started treating them like your nieces and nephew. You've been very standoffish since we took them in. And Sammy sees it as much as Wendy does. Get over yourself and have some fun. Veni? Don't you think we're working on that? That Veni is doing everything in her power to make sure they're taken to jail? Christ, she has a list of things a mile long that she's going to hit them with. When the time is right. They have this one thing they must do before she feels it's time. Do you see me stressing? No, you don't. And you want to know why? What the hell am I going to add to any of this if I'm stressed out? Nothing. Not one damned thing. Only to make my kids stressed and my wife. This is the most useful I've felt in a very long time. And there you sit with your pouty face on, stressing like you're the only one that has issues. Straighten up, or fucking get up and go home. My daughter wants to go to this auction with us tomorrow, but she's afraid to ask you. Did you know that? And you want to know why she's afraid of you?"

"I'm a jackass." Leslie told him he'd gotten it in one. "Is she really afraid to ask me things?"

"Yes. As I said, she didn't even want me to ask you. Sammy just wants you to hug him, but as I said, for the last few days, you've been so bitchy that no one has bothered being around you. If I were you, I'd get my shit together before Hanna does it for you. If she figures out you're making my kids afraid of you, I think she'll have your head for dinner one night." Carroll stretched his neck. "That's another thing you want to stop doing around others. Especially the kids. Stretching out like you just did shows your cat, and he looks as grumpy as you are."

"I'm sorry." Leslie told him he'd better be saying that to the others. "I will. Or better yet, I'll make it up to the kids tonight when we get there. And I'd love to— I'll talk to Wendy too. She's a great kid. I have a feeling she would have only put up with me for a few more hours before she did me in. I'm truly sorry, Leslie. I really am."

"I'm sorry too." Carroll asked him why he was. "Because you felt as if you had to take this on all by yourself. And that you didn't feel like you could come and talk to me about it before I had to resort to violence."

"It's not like that. I swear. I was just being my usual stupid self. I won't let it happen again." Carroll picked up one of the flavorful rolls and bit into it. "I need to relax more."

The two of them enjoyed their lunch, and Leslie could see that Carroll was indeed feeling better about whatever was bothering him. Not telling Veni about Wendy going with him and his brother, Leslie was going to let his brother manage that. Things were looking up. He supposed there was always room for something else to come up, but he was happy now.

~*~

The room was beautiful. To know that the others had done this for her and Leslie made it all the more special. They had been groping one another for the last three days every opportunity they got. Now they were going to have sex, and she was more than just a little bit ready for him. When he finally came into the room, she just stared at him. The man was much too beautiful to be called handsome. There was so much more to him than just looks.

"What are you thinking about right now? The reason I ask is because you have a look on your face that makes me think my poor body is going to be abused. In the best sort of way." She said that was just what she was thinking. "Good. I hope to Christ my brother keeps the kids in his room. That'll give us an entire four walls to make noises through before he can make fun of me tomorrow."

"I have no plans of letting him *not* hear us." Leslie grinned at her. More like he leered at her. "I'm going to be honest with you. All this touching and groping one another when we were close enough has put me on edge. I bet if you were to suddenly be naked, I'd come just from seeing you."

"You mean like this?" It happened, just like she'd joked about. Falling to her knees, she let the climax roll over her. When Leslie wrapped his hand around his thick, dripping cock, she crawled to him so she could have a taste of him.

"You touch me with your mouth, Veni, and I'm going to join you on the floor. Christ almighty."

She could taste his need as if it were her own. Even as needy as she was at the moment, she knew he was even more so. Licking him from root to tip, she swirled her tongue around his crown until Leslie was fucking her mouth like a powerful animal.

Leslie held her head to him. Not that it was much of a hardship in having his cock touching the back of her throat — it was amazing — but he was slowing her down, keeping her sucking on his cock at a slow, steady pace. Sliding her fingers down her breast, over her nipples, she nearly came again when he came a little in her mouth.

"Baby, I don't want to hurt you. Sit there and let me come all over you before I take you to the bed. If you don't, it's nearly going to be over before we begin." She moved back from him, opening her mouth and waiting for his cum to touch her. "That's it, Veni. Taste me."

He cried out when the first drop of his cum hit her breasts. Rubbing the hot cream into her breast, she watched him as he jerked himself off. It was the sexiest thing she'd ever seen. Even her not getting her own rocks off, watching him was like watching every porn movie ever made.

He came so many times on her. Her body was covered in him. Her face, breasts, and tongue were so hot with his cum. When she brushed her fingers over her clit, she came powerfully; nearly taking her under it was so powerful. Seconds after her second climax, Veni found herself on her back, her legs wrapped around Leslie's hips, being fucked hard.

"Come again." She did, bowing her back off the floor. The need to be tighter around him, to have their bodies as one, nearly had her pushing him over so she could fuck him. When he kissed her savagely, she dug her nails into his back and felt the fur of his cat. Screaming out his name, telling them both to make her come, Veni felt the long claws of his leopard digging deeply into her flesh until she was sure they would be found dead this way.

Coming again and again, she was weak with it. Her body was rubber. However, when he turned her over, sitting her up, so her knees were under her, Leslie leaned over her body while he fucked her this way and bit deeply into her shoulder. He dug nails or claws down her back until she came several more times. Even as weak as she was, begging him to stop, he fucked her over and over until she simply let go and slipped away.

When she woke up, she was in the big bed with Leslie beside her, eating some cheese and crackers. As soon as he saw she was awake, he made her several of the little snacks and fed them to her.

"I thought I'd broken you." She told him she was sure he had. "I'm sorry about that. I was…. Christ, I have no words for how it made me feel to watch you make yourself come. Are you sore still? When I picked you up to put you in the bed, you cried out. I'm so very sorry I was too rough on you."

She tried to sit up in bed and didn't hide her pain from him. Veni was sore, all over her entire body. When she was able to sit up on her own without crying, Leslie went to the bathroom to run her a nice bath.

Veni had never been a person who enjoyed baths. She wasn't even sure how she'd like this one. But almost as soon as her bottom touched the tub filled with warm water, she knew this was going to be her best bet in dealing with the pain. Leslie slipped into the tub behind her and wrapped his hands around her to adjust her.

"I have two things to tell you. Nothing

earth-shattering, but you should know. Carroll talked with Wendy, and she is very thrilled to have an uncle she's not afraid of. Also, Sammy has nightmares. I think the only reason we didn't know that before is because Wendy has been getting up with him rather than letting us know about them. Hanna said he's terrified of being left behind. She couldn't tell left where or why, but that's all his jumbled thoughts were about. I'm thinking we need to get him someone to talk to about them that knows how to deal with this kind of trauma." She asked if she should go get him. "No. If you do that, because I wanted to do the same thing, Carroll seems to think he'll be ten times more embarrassed. He's going to talk to him at breakfast in the morning."

Leslie washed her hair as he told her about the auction tomorrow. Then when he rinsed the soap out, she must have dozed a little because again, she woke in the big bed. This time, however, she was alone. Sitting up to see where he'd gone, she saw that it was nearly noon, and she'd been asleep for nearly twelve hours. Getting up, she nearly fell back when she felt every bruise, pulled muscle, and ache throughout her whole body. Veni thought for sure that even her hair hurt. Reaching out to Morgan, she told her how sorry she was.

I'm just glad you got some rest. It's been a few days since either you or Leslie slept well. Children will do that to you. Her face heated up when she realized Morgan more than likely knew just why she'd fallen asleep so late. When she spoke again, she knew it. *Leslie was whistling when he left here earlier. They were both dressed up like they were headed to a corporate meeting. And Wendy looked so smart too. You should have seen her, Leslie. She had a notebook and paper. I think she's going to fit well into this family for things like this. Don't you?*

She finished talking to Morgan as she got out of the shower. Not wanting to disturb anyone at the auction, she asked her new mother-in-law if she'd heard anything. So far, she said she hadn't. But they were having fun.

I told them not to let me know if things are selling or not. I don't want to know until it's all over. Veni said she didn't either. *Good, we're of like minds on this. I just want to have enough to make the used appliance store work for Leslie and to have enough left over to start on my newest project.*

I'm sure you'll have plenty for that. Morgan said they didn't need the money to do either project, but she thought this would be a good way to fund them both. *I agree. It's like finding money in an old coat you haven't worn in a while. I tell myself right up until I'm about to spend it that it's fun money. Usually, I just end up putting it in my cookie jar until – that's where it is. Oh, Morgan, I just remembered where I had hidden the thumb drive I'd taken out the day before they dumped me on the roadside. It's in my money cookie jar. I need to go get it.*

Send Hale after it. He'll be there and back before you could make any kind of arrangements to fly there. Also, no one will be the wiser that he's been there and gone. She said she'd send him now. *Good girl. I'd not be able to have any fun with you if you were worried about getting that drive. Oh, this is wonderful. We're not that far from the hotel if you'd like to join us for lunch. Just come to the table with us. You'll not miss us – we're a lot of people crammed into a large dining room all to ourselves.*

Veni made it there in record time. The more she moved around, the less she ached. As soon as she got to the table, Sammy came to sit by her, and Bethy wanted her. When the little girl called her Momma, Veni was shocked and happy to her very core. Hugging both kids, she helped them order, and the three of them enjoyed being together. She only hoped that Wendy was having as much fun as she had hoped. Also that she wasn't any trouble for the two men.

Chapter 4

"Do we know any more than we did two weeks ago about Venetia? Like where the hell she is? Is she even alive?" Benson said he had no idea on any of those questions as yet. "Why the hell not? Christ, do you have any idea how much is riding on this for us? Not only will we be in trouble with every country we've been taking money from for orders, but the locals aren't going to be all that thrilled about having us loose and on the run, either. Where the fuck is she? And if she had all the information on us, why isn't anyone arresting us right now? The stress over this is killing me. I'll have you know. Just find some answers. Please?"

"I've people everywhere looking for her, Colton. Ten miles in both directions of where she was dropped on the side of the road. That would include any farmland they can search, as well as hotels, hospitals…hell, even vet offices. Nothing." He asked about her house. "Her mail is at the post office, so I have no way of getting into it to see if anyone is asking about her. The house is being watched twenty-four/seven. I have people at restaurants, as well as local hangouts for kids. I tell you, it's like she disappeared off the face of the earth. Except for that man telling us she's still alive, I don't have any way of verifying it either."

"So we're just supposed to wait for someone to arrest us? Bullshit. I'm going to go away for a while. At least until she surfaces either way. Dead or alive." He went to his bedroom to pack. Of course, Benson followed him. "I don't want to go to prison. Because I know as surely as I'm standing here, we're not going to get any kind of break for anything we might say or do to the other. I'm not saying I'd turn you in, Benson. But you have to admit we'd just be digging our own holes deeper with everything else we've done. I'm going to leave the country, and you should do the same. Do you have any cash you can use?"

"Yes. When we started this, if you'll

remember, I was the one that suggested we keep a car, as well as money close at hand to use." He agreed with his longtime friend that he'd loved the idea then, and more so now. "Where are you going? Before you answer that, I should tell you not to tell me. The less we tell each other after this minute, the better off we might be."

"I think that's an excellent idea. Yes, I do." He stuffed everything he thought he'd need to leave the country into his bag, including the passports he'd had made up a few decades ago. "I'm glad I had these updated recently. I'd hate to have to explain why I look so different than twenty years plus ago."

When Colton left him to get his own packing done, Benson put all the things he'd put into the smaller case into the largest one he had. As he was just zipping it closed, his wife returned from her hair appointment. Without a word to her, she realized what they were doing and started packing too. Then she told him to fuck it and just to pack a carry-on full of money.

"Whatever we need, we'll just get it there. I mean, it's not like we're going to have to find us a place to stay. This way, we can have a lovely time and not have to be bothered with credit cards right away." He agreed with her and asked if he should tell Benson. "No. Why would you want to? If he gets his luggage scanned and they find money, he'll be arrested. They don't scan carry-on's, do they?" He didn't know. Did they?

As they were putting their things into the car, he decided something else. If he were to buy his ticket with his wife, then it would look like they were running. After telling her his plan, she grabbed him by the throat and pulled him to her so that he was looking into her eyes.

"You fuck me over, Benson Applegate, I will throw you under the bus. I don't mean figuratively either. Your ass will be crushed, along with that fucking empty head of yours." He swore to her that he'd not ever once thought of leaving her to be the fall guy. "Good. You keep realizing that we're partners, and you might just live long enough to have some fun."

If he told himself every day that his wife was scary, he'd still be surprised by her every day. She wasn't one to mess with, and worse than that, she would follow through on her promises to hurt or kill you too. Shivering at the memory of the look in her eyes just now, Benson dumped everything on the bed and picked up his carry-on to use.

He'd met his partner in law school. Neither

of them was doing all that well, and since money was easy to come by, especially since they lived on campus then, they bought their education. No one would hire them, of course. That was why forming a partnership with each other had worked out so well. Also, it was a nice safe place for them to talk about what they wanted to do once their projects got up and off the ground. It hadn't taken them very long to get enough money to purchase a home, security, as well as having the finer things in life right at their fingertips.

They got richer as the years went on. Of course, they spent money like it was always going to be there at first. Then when they met their wives and gotten married, their wives had made sure that not only was there money to run with, but there would be a home waiting for them so they'd not have to go without. Not that he had asked if Colton had the same thing going on with his run money. He just assumed since their wives were so close that they'd come up with the idea together. He asked his wife about it.

"I did not tell her. As far as our friendship goes, we only stuck around together because of the two of you. If she had any ideas about anything, she never shared. Nor did I with her.

It was easier to talk about upcoming events that we'd be in rather than to try and talk about money. Again, if they didn't make preparations, then they have no one to blame but themselves." He kissed her on the cheek. "What was that for?"

"For being the best wife in the world. My goodness, I don't know where I'd be without you there for me. Not to mention how broke I'd be. You've single-handedly gotten me out of several sticky situations, and I couldn't love you more for it." She told him he knew who buttered his biscuits. "Yes. I guess you did."

He was still chuckling about what she'd said when they were both in separate lines at the gates to get their flight information. The kiosks made it very nice to be able to buy a ticket without anyone talking to him. Also, he loved the fact that his wife had reminded him to get out his passport before he got out of the car. That way, he'd not be fumbling with it in line. Such a smart woman he had found.

He still had to stand in line, but he took that time to observe people. He didn't care for them as a whole. However, he enjoyed watching them when they thought no one was noticing them as they fought with their other half. Or their children. The old saying about a person being smart but people were stupid had rang true. Even in the airport they were in, it seemed to him they got dumber the closer they were to leaving the place. He saw one person he knew but ignored them for staying in line. Benson decided he should have done this days ago. The place was buzzing with cops.

The money had been just where he had put it. Sometimes he'd take some of the running money and put it in a stash. Then his wife would come along, hide it in a better place, and write it in the book. However, the first place they had gone to get it had been cleaned out. Scaring him a bit, he was thrilled when the next four had proved to be filled, just as he'd thought they should have been. If they ever got rid of lockers at bus stations, he didn't know what he'd do.

"Next." He moved up to the counter and smiled at the woman there. Handing over his ticket as well as his passport to the woman, he didn't bother with chit chat. One thing he'd learned was that they didn't care for it, as they heard it all day long, and he didn't want to engage with her in the event he made himself stand out for her to remember him. "It says here that you're going to France."

"Yes." It wasn't a question, he realized,

until after answering her. Waiting for her to give his things back, Benson looked around. There was a commotion down the way, and it seemed that every cop in the place was on their way there. Seeing his wife, he didn't bother trying to figure it out. She was all right, and he was as well.

"Next."

He had his things back in his pocket and was headed down to the part of the airport where they'd be nearer to the gates. Passing his wife as she stood in line at the counter to get herself some coffee, he thought that another wonderful idea. Stopping at the next one, he got himself a large tea. Enjoying himself, he was seated before she was and fixed up his cup with sugar and cream.

A person sat down next to him — too close, he thought — and Benson scooted away. But the man moved next to him again, this time spilling not only his tea but also jostling his arm, so his hand was burnt.

"What are you doing? Watch it there. I have hot tea here." The man took the cup from him and tossed it, with one try, right into the container across from him. If he wasn't so upset with what he'd just done, Benson might well have been impressed. Sometimes he couldn't hit the trashcan even if he was standing over it.

"You're going to go get me another one, or I'll tell the police."

The man only leaned back in the seat and opened his jacket. The letters FBI were right there for him to see. Benson grabbed his bag and started to rise when the man shoved something that felt like a gun into his ribs.

"If you sit here nicely, then I won't have to kill you where you're sitting. Just wait for a moment here, and you'll see a show." He didn't want to see a fucking show. He wanted to escape. But the man nodded to his left, and that was where he looked. "You see, that is why you should never run. Applegate and his wife were not nearly as slick as you were, but they were still caught. Why is it that people run anyway? Don't you think that with all the computers around, we'd be able to locate you without any trouble? Even you using a fake passport didn't help you. We have facial recognition that will connect you to any name you try to use."

He watched as Colton was being dragged, literally, from someplace further down the lane, with his wife screaming at the top of her lungs about how they had the wrong people. When Colton said he knew where he was, Benson could have killed the man for what he was screaming to the others.

"He's taking off too. I know he is because he told me. Benson has money too. More than I do, and he's running with it. His wife is a smart cookie, so I know he more than likely has a house someplace that he can go to as well." On and on Colton went until he was no longer close enough for him to hear. Benson looked at the Fed.

"You might want to have a look where your wife is currently being arrested. She's not singing yet, but she will. The first words out of her mouth about you were that she was going to fucking kill you." He laughed. "I do believe she thinks you turned her in. Of course, it might be what was said to her when they cuffed her. The two who arrested her said they'd have to thank you for your help in this arrest. I don't know for sure. But then, I got the pleasure of arresting you."

He was taken in. Benson didn't bother trying to get away, nor did he try to cut himself a deal. Keeping his mouth shut would go a long way in making sure he wasn't somehow dead before he got to the jail. Or wherever they were taking him. Sitting in the back of the van, cuffed to the floor, he wondered yet again where that fucking cunt Venetia was. He knew on some level—

"Hello, Benson. It's been a long time, don't you think? However, if you were hoping you'd not see me again because you killed me, then you're in for even more surprises than me showing up here." Benson asked her why she was bothering him. "It's what I live for. To bother you. And to have you go to prison for not just trying to kill me, but my biological parents, as well as the people who raised me. I led the Feds right to their graves. You and Colton are going away for a very long time."

"I don't even care anymore." Venetia pouted at him. "You'd think I made you suffer or something by the way you've brought all this down on us. You were supposed to have died quickly. Then you just disappeared. Where the hell did you go, anyway?"

"I found my mate. My husband. We are in the process of adopting three of the most wonderful children too." He shivered. Benson did that every time he thought of children. "You don't like kids? That's sad. When they hug you, it's like you've been given a second chance on—"

"Why are you here, Venetia? Did you have something to add to the list I'm sure you've given them about myself and Colton? If so, I think you've done quite enough. Go away." She explained to him about the thumb drive. "You actually kept records of the shit you saw going on at my offices? Christ, have you no loyalty to those that employ you? What the fuck, Venetia? That's just not right."

"Neither was trying to kill my parents." He asked her what she meant. "They're not dead. Didn't I mention that? Oh well, they're with the Feds now too. Seems they have a beef about you shooting them and leaving them for dead. They might well have been if not for my sister. You knew I had one, didn't you?"

"No." When she didn't say anything else, he decided he was going to prison anyway. Why not just spill it all to her. "Did you talk to your father about why we killed or tried to kill him? He could touch things and know all about them. Like evidence from a crime scene and where a shipment was coming from. He could have been wealthy. But no, he had to go all good citizen on us and decided to turn us in. Like you, he should have died that day. Your mother too. She wouldn't have been hurt too badly if she'd just allowed me to fuck her once or twice. She actually got all uppity and thought that telling my wife, Sharon, would end it. But that backfired. Sharon wanted to watch me fuck your pretty little mother."

She only smiled at him. Benson wanted her pissed off. Wanted her to lash out at him. Perhaps kill him so he'd not have to go through a trial, then prison. But she only continued to smile at him. Pissy now, he asked her if she was a simpleton.

"Hardly. I'm not only a good deal smarter than you and your partner would ever hope to be, but I'm exactly like my father. He's a warlock. I'm a witch. A very powerful one, as a matter of fact. More so than even my older sister that you didn't know about." He said he didn't believe her. "Be that as it may, I am."

When she put out her hand, he flinched back from her. Her laughter reminded him of her dad, and when she thanked him for that, he wanted to kick her. He didn't because as soon as the thought entered his head, she showed him just how powerful she really was.

"This is your wife. I'm sorry to let you find out she was dead this way, but I didn't know." He told her that wasn't funny. "I'm not being funny, Benson. But she is dead. It looks like she was shot about five times before they stopped. Let me adjust the color for you."

The blood was still pooling around her

head when the colors were adjusted. Not only had she been shot five times, as Venetia said, but they'd all gotten her in the head. Her hair, always so neat and well taken care of was a mess of blood and knots. Her forehead was nearly blown off her head, and the look on her face told him she didn't feel the bullets entering her but had still been in mid-tirade when she'd been killed.

"Why did they kill her?" Venetia said she didn't know, as she had only just found out when he had. "What about Colton? And his wife, Libby? How are they faring in all this?"

"Libby is dead as well, I'm afraid. Colton doesn't look as if he's going to make it. He tried to run after seeing you in the lobby being escorted out." Both of their deaths were shown to him, and he didn't know what he felt about the two of them being dead. His heart was broken because his Sharon was gone.

"What happens now? Do I still go to prison?" She asked him why he thought he'd not be going to prison. "I don't know. Grief for my wife being dead. Will they cut me some slack?"

"I'd not count on it if I were you. You didn't cut anyone else any slack when you killed them, did you?" He hadn't. He knew that. "Well,

I'm going to leave you here to face the rest of your life, Benson. You behave yourself in prison, or things will go badly for you." She winked at him. "It will too. I can see that."

Benson was left to his own heartbreak. Even as he sobbed for his loss, he knew this was just what he should have expected. When someone got into the back of the van with him, Benson didn't bother engaging in any conversation. It was just too much for him. How could they have killed his wife? was all he could think about right now.

~*~

Wendy couldn't have had more fun if her very life depended on it. Not only did she get to watch the bidders that wanted the gems being displayed, but she also got to take notes on things she'd change if given the chance. While she knew she was just a kid and no one would take her seriously, she still wrote down her observations as if it were a homework assignment and she was going to be graded on it. Dad, what she decided to call Leslie from now on, asked her if she was ready to go.

"Yes. Did you make enough money?" He laughed like he had lost his mind for a moment, then closed his mouth and nodded. "You're wigged out, aren't you?"

"I am, as a matter of fact. We made a great deal of money. Even after the auction house takes their cut, we're going to have more money than we can spend over several hundred lifetimes. How did your notes go?" She showed him what she'd done. "These are really good suggestions, Wendy. You should show them to Mr. Martin."

"No. I just did this for my own pleasure." But before she could put them away, back into her small backpack, Dad was calling for Mr. Martin and asking him if he had a few minutes for his daughter to talk to him. "It's all right if you don't. Really. Dad is making a big deal out of nothing."

"I have all the time in the world for you, young lady. What is it you wish to show me?" Dad handed the notes to the man, and he sat down in the seat behind him. She liked that he was being kind to her. Really, who was going to take the notes of a kid when this place was making so much money? "These are wonderful suggestions. I love the one where you said that a closed caption-like camera needs to be set up so people can have better views of the object. That would have been helpful today. How would it work for the patrons?"

"Each seat would have a small monitor. They'd be attached to the table so they can look at them and not be able to take them. I'm not sure why anyone would take a small device when they spend as much money as some of these people do. But they'd be able to zoom in and see some of the pictures in the catalog too." He asked about having them built into the table. "I thought of that too, but the lighting in here is too much for them. At least this way, they'd be able to shade them, so there isn't any glare. Which brings me to something I didn't write down. You have too much going on in this room to make the things you are selling look good."

"Someone said that to me before. That it's too busy." She nodded and looked at Dad. At his nod, she told Mr. Martin that he needed the walls to be white, as well as plants in the corners. "Plants? Well, I guess that wouldn't hurt any. What about the seating here? All you have written down is the seating is like the lunchroom at school."

They talked for an hour about her notes and suggestions. He seemed to be listening to her, and at one point, even took one of her other note pads and began making his own notes. Mr. Martin loved the idea of all white in the room.

And to put the windows much higher in the room so there would be no distractions from traffic outside. By the time they were finished with her notes, Mr. Martin had three pages more than she did on her pad. He was taking her suggestions and adding anything else she had to say about the notes.

"My goodness, you've no idea how much I'm going to enjoy getting this started. If you have the time over the next couple of days while you're here, perhaps you can look at the other two rooms we have to use. One of the rooms is smaller than this one by half, and the second room is a media room. That sounds more pretentious than it really is. It's where we have online auctions. It's just for bids coming in over the lines." She said she'd have to talk to her parents. "Of course you will. Good girl."

When they were headed out into the sunshine, she had to sit down. It was overwhelming for her to have someone listen to what she had to say. While she was sitting there, Carroll sat down next to her and smiled.

"You are brilliant. I hope you know that." She only nodded at him, still not sure what he felt about her. "I also wanted to apologize to you about how I've been acting around you and your brother. It wasn't you. It was pointed out to me that I have no reason to be stressed, and I was stressing myself out all on my own and not being there for you in a way that you could come and talk to me."

"You hurt my brother's feelings." He said he knew that and was more than sorry for that. "Did my dad hit you? You said it was pointed out to you. I'm assuming it was him or your wife. Nah, now that I think about it, it couldn't have been Aunt Hanna. She would have hurt you, so it showed."

"Your dad hit me." He laughed when she did. "Not that I didn't deserve it, but he made his point. I'm truly sorry, Wendy. I didn't mean for you to feel like I wasn't happy you are a part of this family. Also, I'm hoping you'll be our babysitter when our child is born."

"For money?" He laughed and said, of course. "Then good. I'll do it. I also need a favor from you. If you don't mind. I'd ask my parents, but they tend to go a little overboard about things when we ask for them. Not in a really bad way, but I would like to have a computer in my room, with a printer. I want to take some online classes, and if I ask them for it, they'll have me outfitted with all the best things, and all I want is a computer and a printer. I don't need a filing cabinet or anything like that. Just those two things."

"You want me to buy them for you?" Wendy just glared at him. "I'll take that as a no. I'll see what I can do about talking with them for one."

Mr. Martin came out of the building and smiled. "I'm so glad I was able to catch you, Wendy. Your dad is finishing up the paperwork for the sale, and he'll be out directly. But this is your check for the work you did for me this afternoon. I'm going to take all your suggestions and make them work. I feel that with your help, I might be big enough to make that expansion I have been thinking about. Thank you very much." Then he left them there.

Wendy wasn't sure this was a good idea, but with Uncle Carroll's encouragement, she opened the envelope. Handing it over to him, he was laughing so hard that she jerked the check back from him to read the numbers again. Mr. Martin had paid her a hundred thousand dollars for making a few notes on her notepad.

"I think it's safe to say you can purchase your own computer." Wendy glared at him once again. "My goodness. I think you just found your own way to make money. And good money too. Congratulations, Wendy, and welcome to the corporate world."

She was going to murder him. Not that she had any idea how to go about that, but she'd give it some thought. The man was laughing at her because she'd gotten money. Or perhaps, she thought, she'd tell Aunt Hanna. That would surely make him behave himself. Maybe. He seemed to like making Aunt Hanna upset so he could laugh at her. Men were stupid, Wendy thought. Stupid and dumb.

Dad showed her and his brother the money. There were three checks, each of them with so many zeros, she had to ask what the amount was. They were both laughing as they explained to her not only the amount but why there were three checks. Wendy decided she was going to have a nice little sit down with Grandma Morgan. She'd make sure they treated her better after that.

Meeting up with the rest of the family, she didn't know what to do with the money that was hers. Instead of showing off, which was something she didn't ever do, she asked her grandma to hold onto it for her. As soon as she saw what the amount was for on the check, she hugged her and told her how proud she was of her.

It was a really nice feeling having someone proud of you, Wendy thought. She'd never had her parents tell her anything close to what her new family had done today for her. She wondered if there was ever a time when either of them had expressed those words to anyone. Not thinking about that now, she enjoyed her dinner with the family. She was going to work for Mr. Martin, but what he'd paid her was more than enough. It was also good to have someone value her. Wendy had never felt this good before, and she was happy to have someone love her.

Chapter 5

Sammy was having fun in the yard. He'd never had a place where he could just sit in the grass and watch the trees go back and forth. It was relaxing. It was something he'd been doing since they'd come back from New York three days ago.

Just as he was closing his eyes to take a nap, he heard a commotion. Sammy wasn't entirely sure what that word meant, but his Grandma Morgan said it a lot, and he'd been trying it out for himself. Looking around, he didn't see anything until he saw two big dogs chasing something near the tree line.

He wasn't stupid, thinking he could take on two large dogs, but as soon as he saw Mr. Weeds, he knew he had to do something. Picking up a huge stick, he started swatting it at the dogs to make them back off. Once they were back far enough, he put Mr. Weeds into his shirt pocket and tried his best to run them off. The dogs were not having it.

"Faeries? I need some help." He screamed it two more times before they came to help him. "They've hurt Mr. Weeds. Can you keep them from coming after me while I find him some help? I don't know how hurt he is, but I know he's bleeding."

Before he could get to the house with the little gnome, the dogs were running off. Two more faeries came to join him on the deck as he pulled the little man from his pocket. It was much worse than he'd thought.

"What can I do to help him? He's my friend." Pixie, one of the several faeries that had come to help him, told him to call on Tellus. "I don't know how to do that. Please, we have to save him."

Mr. Weeds' body had been bitten several times. His beard was full of blood too. What scared him the most was that his leg looked like it had been nearly torn off. Crying a little but still talking to the little man, he did what he was told to call on Tellus.

"Come to me, Mother of the Earth. I need your help for one of your own." When Pixie nodded to him as he stood in the middle of the yard with his shoes off, he decided to tell her more. "Hurry, please. Mr. Weeds is in terrible shape."

"Let me have a look at him, young Sammy." The woman just appeared in front of him, and he put out his hands to show her his friend. "My goodness. He is in bad shape. I believe I can help him, but I shall need your help."

"Anything. You need me to give you my life. I'll do it. He's been the best friend I could ever have. I love him." Tellus said she'd only need a drop of his blood but was proud of him for being willing to sacrifice himself for such an important person. "He's important to me too. Mr. Weeds showed me how to relax and listen to the world around me. I owe him everything, as he talked me out of taking my own life."

"Oh no, child. Never think that." She pulled a blade from the air and handed it to him. "Just cut the tip of your finger, any one of them will do, and give the blood to him. Then put a drop or two on his leg as well."

Sammy didn't question her about anything but did what she wanted. The drops of blood to his legs was first because he was still bleeding from there. He also put some of his blood on his other leg when he noticed that it too was injured. Mr. Weeds needed Sammy's help to open his mouth so that Sammy could give him the blood.

As they both sat there watching him, Sammy noticed that there were a great many other creatures around than there had been before. Some of them were thanking him for saving such a man, while others were offering Sammy gifts for his quick thinking to save their Mr. Weeds.

Grandma Morgan came out a few minutes later. She said she'd been called to help as well. But once she looked over the gnome, she told him he'd done a very good job, and it looked as if Mr. Weeds would live.

"Will he be able to walk and get around? I know he loves to talk and to go out and see people. I'd hate for him to have to sit at home all the time. He's my friend."

Grandma Morgan said it was difficult to tell right now, but she didn't foresee any trouble.

When the family showed up to keep an eye on Mr. Weeds with him, others came too. David, the king of the underearth, offered roots to dry for their pantry. Holly offered to plant a special garden for him when he was in need of herbs. Everyone was so generous, but all he wanted was for Mr. Weeds to wake up and be well again.

Taking the little man into the house, Sammy put him in a nice box that had been padded with cotton. Keeping an eye on him for the rest of the evening, Sammy was getting worried that he'd not even opened one eye. Then he remembered that Mr. Weeds loved stories. Of all kinds. Especially ones of his life before coming to be with his new parents.

"I never told my sister about this one. She'd have a fit if she ever found out. But one night, I was given a bottle of water by Rebecca to drink down. Wendy showed me this trick when she figured it out. She called it a double distraction. But you couldn't use it more than once. Anyway, I had a new bottle of water under my bed. Knocking her bottle to the floor, I got my bottle and drank it down while Rebecca told me how stupid I was and that she couldn't wait for me to be out of the house. She thought that all of us were going to be eighteen to move out. I would have left that night had I been able to find myself a place to live like this one." He thought about how he'd nearly messed up and picked up the wrong bottle when he'd reached for his.

But that wasn't important right now. "I was pretending to be asleep when she came into my room. I was nearly ready to leap out the window when she came to me and shook me hard. When I didn't open my eyes, she told someone else in the room that I was ready."

Sammy cried when he thought of what had nearly happened to him that night. A stranger had nearly raped him. If not for him switching out the waters, he would surely have died that night. Instead, he pretended to wake up and hit the man with the lamp by his bed. There had been blood everywhere when he'd run out of the house. Wendy followed him out with Bethy, and they hid in the cornfield for two days before they went back to the house. Both of them had been beaten, and Bethy had been drugged up to the point they were sure she was dead a couple of times.

"We should have died a long time ago, I'm thinking now." Sammy thought of the night Mr. Weeds had come to his room when he'd been figuring out how to slice his wrists and kill himself. "You saved me that night, Mr. Weeds. Even helping you now isn't enough for what you did for me. Samuel didn't care one way or the other what Rebecca was doing to us so long as he didn't have to be bothered about us. I was depressed in thinking I'd never be loved in all my life. You came to me and showed me the little things this family was doing for us to make sure we were not just safe but were loved and taken care of. Without you coming to me, I would have killed myself and not ever thought that I'd been loved. I can't thank you enough for all you did for me in that few minutes."

"You are worthy, young man, and you're never to forget that." Sammy cried and laughed at the same time when Mr. Weeds spoke to him. He still looked terrible, but he could see that his leg was nearly healed, and his body, where he'd been bitten, was healing too. He asked him how he was feeling. "Like a couple of wild dogs nearly had me for dinner. How are you? You didn't take them on, did you? My goodness, they were mean dogs."

He told him how he'd called for the faeries to help him and that Tellus had come to help as well. Sammy even admitted that he'd been terrified for not just him but himself as well. Mr. Weeds fell back to sleep then, telling him he had to rest a bit more. Sammy was so relieved the man was going to live that he laid down beside him and fell asleep himself.

When he woke, Mr. Weeds was sitting on the side of the bed staring at him. Smiling at the gentleman, Sammy asked him how he was feeling. A quick nod had Sammy sitting up as well and stretching like he'd been saving it up for a long time.

"You did a good thing in saving me, son." Sammy said he was his friend. "Yes, I am at that. You're mine too. But you did a good thing not just for the two of us, but for the world as well."

"I never thought of that when I saw you being hurt, Mr. Weeds. I know I should have, but all I could think about was that those dogs were hurting you — maybe even killing you — and you were my best friend." Mr. Weeds asked him if he could now please call him Thad. "I could, I guess, but it sure will be weird."

They both laughed, and he took Thad down to the kitchen with him. He could get around very well, but there was no point in him being worn out so soon. As soon as the two of them were seated, Grandma Morgan sat with him. She said she had something important to tell him.

"The other kings and queens of the land wish to thank you for saving the king of gnomes. He is, as I'm sure you understand now, an important part of what goes on, not only on this land but all the lands. All the gnomes are grateful to you as well." Shyly he looked at Thad, then back at his grandma. "What is it, Sammy? Something I can help you with?"

"I don't know what he does. And I don't really care. He's my friend, and I only saved him because I know he'd do the same for me." Grandma Morgan patted him on his hand, then stood up to go to the sink. He knew he'd upset her and was sorry for that. "I didn't mean to say the wrong thing, Grandma. I truly didn't. Thad, he told me I could call him that, has been a good friend to me and teaching me all sorts of things that make this land work so well for all of us. If I upset you, I'm so sorry."

"You didn't upset me, Sammy. You said the exact thing that Leslie said you would. That it mattered little to you that you'd be thought of as a hero. You only did it to save a friend. I'm so very proud of you for that. And the others, their gifts to you, will be so much nicer for that simple reason." He told her he didn't want any gifts. "I would think you'd not. But to refuse even one of them would be an insult to everyone that comes here. You understand that, don't you?"

"No. But I believe you, so I'll take them."

He looked at Thad, then back at his new grandma. "I can share them with my sisters, can't I? They won't care too much, will they, if I share? I can give some of the gifts to my sisters and not upset them, don't you think?"

"Yes, Sammy. They'll be very happy to know you're willing to share something from each of them. Thank you." He finished his breakfast, then he and Thad started out into the yard. "Be back by noon, all right?"

"Yes, ma'am."

He and Thad visited all the other creatures in the yard. He wanted them to know he was much better, and Thad also wanted to thank the faeries that helped take care of the dogs. They were dead, the dogs, and Sammy found that he didn't care. If his sisters had been in the yard, the mean animals might well have gone after them.

It was nearing noon when the two of them headed back to the house. Hugging his new parents always gave him such a good feeling that he wanted to hug them each and every minute. Sammy knew that would just be silly, but he did love how they treated him and his sisters. Like they'd been their children all along.

Eating a quick lunch of salad with chicken cut up all over it, he was to go to the living room.

Grandma's living room looked like something out of a magazine with all the beautiful flowers all over the room. Plants in every corner were prettied up with lights on some of them. He was seated on the couch when his parents and Tellus joined them.

"Hello, young man. My goodness, you look much better than you did only a few days ago. I'm glad you got some rest." Sammy told the queen he'd been visiting with Thad. "Yes, he told me you were taking good care of him so he'd not overdo it."

"Yes, ma'am." The room tightened up like all the air had been sucked out of it at once. When he started to stand, to get some air, the queen put her hand on his, and he could take a deep breath then. "What was that?"

"They're here." Who? Then he saw them—the most sparkly people he'd ever seen. Even looking at Thad now, along with the queen, they too were sparkling a great deal. It was then he realized that he was in the presence of greatness. These people ran the world, and he didn't think even the president had as much power as any one of them in the room with him. "Are you ready, young man?"

"I suppose so. I maybe should have asked

you, but these gifts, they're not going to hurt me, are they? I don't mind taking them, but I don't want to hurt because I did." Tellus told him he'd be as safe as he'd made Thad. "Okay then. I'm as ready as you are."

"Samuel Peter Canavan Golden, I the Queen Tellus, terrestrial being that cares for and is wholly a part of this earth, I hereby proclaim you as the savior to King Thaddeus Weeds, king of all gnomes of the world." She asked him to sit at the small table that hadn't been there before. "If you would spread out your fingers with your palms up, child, we'll begin."

The kiss to his forehead gave him a tingly feeling, and he felt slightly lightheaded afterwards. But when his mom and dad sat on either side of him with his sisters, Sammy felt like he could take on the world right then. It wasn't a feeling he'd ever had before.

"I'll be rewarding you first, my friend." Nodding, he was glad that Thad was going to be first. "I give to you my friendship. Now, I know what it is you're thinking, that you've had it for a while now. But with my friendship, I also give you the gift of gnomes. All that are living now and all that come to this world will serve you as they serve me. You are now, and forever will be, a gnome of my heart, Sammy."

The small axe, no bigger than one of his new toys, was set upon his thumb. It didn't move but seemed to be stuck to him there. Sammy thought this might be easier than he'd thought. At least no one had hurt him.

The second person, Holly, queen of the landscape realm, was next. "I give to you, Sammy Golden, the gift of the flowers and trees. You will, beyond any other being, be able to understand them and the language they sing to you. I've seen you watching them, swaying to the wind going through their branches. This way, you'll be able to hear their songs and know what they need now and forever."

Sammy was given a drop of water from the king of the waters. With it, he was told that he'd hear and be able to control the waters. Each time a person—king or queen—blessed him with a gift, they would lay a small token on his fingertip before the next person could come forward. By the time they'd all given him something, each of his fingers was filled with some small item that had to do with the gift he'd received.

Then his Grandma Morgan sat before him. "I am Morgan, Queen of the Shifters. I give you the gift of all shifters, Sammy. All shifters in the world were created by me with the magic from the others. I give you their strength, their knowledge, and their ability to become what they need to be. This gift, the ability to shift, you may share with your sisters. But not until you're twelve. You are a survivor, the same as your sisters. You'll grow up to be a good man, a better man than even your own father. And that is saying a great deal because my boys are all good men. You will, with this gift, be able to understand all creatures, the same as me." He watched as she put her thumb into the middle of his right palm. When she lifted her thumb, there was a pawprint there that looked exactly like the one he'd seen on her shoulder one hot afternoon. "You have made me and this household proud by your actions. Thank you."

The next person that sat before him was Hanna. At her wink, he smiled. All she did was touch the middle of his left palm with her thumb as well, but what she left behind was a star. Looking at it as it shimmered in his hand, he watched as it rose above his hand, taking the other gifts with it.

"With my gift, I give you the knowledge of all the other gifts you've been given. You wished to share with your sisters — is that still something you wish to do?" He nodded and asked if his parents could have it as well. "Yes. You're more generous than anyone I've ever encountered, Sammy. Use these gifts for the needs of the others around you, and you will be a man that people everywhere will look up to. A person that creatures will come to for help. Sammy Golden, I give you everything that we have, each of us, for you to keep anyone that needs it safe."

The star continued to spin around, and the gifts he'd been given seemed to be caught up in a tornado. As they started to come together, forming a long spinning line, he watched in fascination as the line split into five lines, then slammed into each of his sisters, himself, and his parents. Sammy lost his hold on his body as he felt as if he'd been torn in two.

~*~

"Did you know it was going to do that?" Hanna told her she hadn't. This time she had a bit of a snark at the end of the word. Veni was still a little pissed off at the other woman, but since she scared her just enough for her not to show it, she kept telling herself that they were all fine. A little dizzy at times, but nothing to show for their actions except for the markings on their palms. "What does this mean to us? I'm sure you know more than you're telling me."

"Nope." Again, she was glad she remembered she was afraid of Hanna, or she might well have punched her in the face. "I'm not sure if you realize this or not, but I can see your anger on your face. I'd not play poker with anyone. You can be read like a book cover. What is it you're wanting to know? Stop asking me the same shit over and over when I've already told you I don't know. Maybe you'll be able to get your panties straightened out, and we can move on. Ask me."

"What did we get?" Hanna turned to her then, and she looked so blank it scared her even more. "I know that something happened. Each of us were knocked out, even Bethy. But they're all fine and out playing in the yard like it was no big deal. I feel like I have something creeping all over my brain, and I can't make it stop."

"Did it occur to you that if you were to just settle down, it would be all right? You're holding up the magic that was given to you. I'm assuming since, as you said, the kids are out playing around that they just let the shit flow over them." Hanna looked at her like she was a bug under a microscope. "You're stubborn, aren't you? I can't help you if you're not willing to help yourself. Let it take hold, Veni. I'm sure that as soon as you do, you'll stop pestering the fuck out of me about what it is that was done to you."

She didn't know how to let it take her. Looking around the deck, she confessed to Hanna something that had been bothering her since she woke up in her bed. When there was no answer from her, Veni turned to see if she'd left or was just ignoring her.

"When I was asked to mix the magic you were to receive, I didn't bother asking why. Then I saw the others giving Sammy his gifts, and I realized what they were doing. The small gifts they put on his fingers were just a distraction for the young kid. The magic they gave him — the gift if you wish to call it — was already his to use. The same with the rest of you." She asked her again why it had knocked them out. "Do you have any idea how powerful any of the people that were there are? I'm including me in that lot. I'm powerful because of getting some magic from Carroll. I also gathered up more as I made my way around the compound and was gifted some from each of the people I encountered. Most of my magic came from the unicorns that live around here. While they let people think there is just the pair of them, there are hundreds of them living here and at the castle of Tellus. The large amount that I was given from them has grown a great deal since then. Also the knowledge of how to use it. Do you know why I know how to use it? Because I let it come to me, and now I'm glad I did. How about you? Along with all this extra magic, you do know that you're the grand witch, right?" She shook her head, and Hanna nodded. "You are. All the other creatures know who you are and what. I thought they were talking about your sister, Zippy. But it's you. You're the grand witch of all witches, and I knew it before you did."

Hanna danced around the room after getting up. Veni had to think hard on what was going on in her mind when Hanna sat down again. Questions seemed to be on a constant loop, but she just sat there. Looking out over the backyard—the view from her windows was amazing—she saw Bethy with Wendy and had to laugh when Sammy was trying his best to do flips to entertain the other two.

"I'm the grand-witch." Hanna didn't comment this time but only nodded. "Christ, no wonder all this is moving around in my mind. Somehow all this got woken up, and I'm buzzing with extra stuff. I'm the fucking grand-witch of all witches. Which will make Leslie the grand warlock. Won't it?"

"I don't know that one. I mean, it would stand to reason, I guess. But since I've never heard of any warlock around, I guess it would be him." Veni told Hanna that her dad was one. "Then he'd be the one to ask. By the way, I removed the bullets from your parents' bodies. I did it a few days ago and forgot to tell you. Your mom had one still in her spine that I think was paining her a great deal. And your father, since someone had already removed one of them, I took the rest of them out. Also did a bit of tweaking to his leg. It was weaker due to him being unable to use it well for the last twenty years."

"Thank you for that. I had thought it had already been taken care of for them. I feel bad now." Hanna told Veni they had understood about her being so busy and that it wasn't any big deal for her to do it. "I shouldn't have been too busy for my parents."

They talked about some things that were going on around town. The things that Morgan had set up long ago and how it was benefiting a great many people. Veni looked at Hanna and realized at that moment, things were happening to her.

"I feel it." She couldn't explain to Hanna what she was feeling because her mind was being overloaded with things she could do. When someone touched her hand and told her to breathe, she knew it was Leslie. "Hold me."

"I am. You're doing fine." He spoke to her through the entire download. There was no other word to describe what she was feeling. When it seemed to settle, not stop, she could finally open her eyes as the kaleidoscope of colors she could see was gone. "How you doing? Better now?"

"Yes. I was talking to Hanna and was distracted. I believe now that I say that, it was her plan. Anyway, she— Where did she go?" He told her she wanted to talk to someone for a minute. "Yes, she more than likely has gone to talk to my dad and see if he's the grand-warlock to my grand witch. Did you know I was?"

"I didn't give it any thought. But now that you mention it, I think you might well be right. I have some news for you if you're okay enough to hear it." She nodded. "The barn is now full of whatever second hand appliances we could find. There are quite a few new ones in there too that the faeries have 'damaged' a bit to make them look used."

"What about the couple that is going to run the place for you? Are they settled in as well?" Leslie told her they were so excited to be living there that they were having a party tomorrow night to celebrate with their family. This house seemed to be much safer for them all to be in. "That's wonderful. I bet it makes you feel good when you do something like that. I have a new list running through my own head that I want to get a start on. Oh, I nearly forgot. Your brother Marley is looking for you. He said it was important that he speak to you, but not to make a big deal about it. I asked him if I could help him, and he kissed me on the nose. Does that work often for you guys?"

"Not usually, no. But I'll tell him that I'm here with you." She got up then to make some lunch for the kids. "Mom wants to know if it would be all right with you if she feeds the kids lunch through the week. She said it gives her time to get to be with them. I believe your parents are going to be there to get to know them as well. I told her I didn't think it would be a problem but that I would tell you."

"That's wonderful. I can see Morgan making sure they eat good things while my parents will be trying to slip them something sweet. Did you know that Zippy is opening a shop not far from here?" Leslie told her he knew where the shop was, and he had known about it. "I'm glad for her. She really enjoys being around people, and I can't think of a better setting for her to do that. Want to take a walk? I have an urge to take a walk into town to have a look around. I'll even let you buy me lunch if you've not eaten."

"I've not and would love to do that. If you don't mind if Marley joins us." She said she didn't mind at all. "Good. He's going to meet us there, but we're not to say aloud what he's telling us. I don't know what is going on, but he's really upset about something."

They walked to the ice cream shop that had seating indoors. Leslie was telling her that up until about four years ago, it was just outdoor seating. But when the owner asked them for a loan to expand, their mom had told him what she thought would work for him. Just recently, he was asking for another loan to expand once again.

They talked about the shop, along with other shops that had recently wanted to expand. "We'll go over their records for the shop they want to work on, as well as the reasons for the expansion. Mom told us that everyone wants a bigger piece of the pie, but she's very careful not to give money to anyone that hasn't proven their need." She asked if it was because they'd not be able to pay her back. "No. Mom doesn't want them using the money they make to pay her back quicker rather than using it for their own families. We've had that happen before. She won't lend money to someone that is very close to closing up, either. It's not what we are here for."

Marley joined them just as their food, his too, was brought out to them. It always surprised her when they'd order so much for themselves. But they ate it, and that, she supposed, was all that mattered. The beef for the burgers, she'd found out recently, was from the Morgan Leap. As were most of the veggies that were used here.

She's not my mate. Leslie looked at her, then at his brother as he spoke to them. *Let me explain. As best I can, anyway.*

Chapter 6

"I was in the barn last night. Not really in there for any real reason, but I was standing at the back of the barn when I heard someone enter the front. If there hadn't been a warning from Danish, I would have called out and not been privy to what Piper and her mother had to say." It was Veni that asked him if he really wasn't Piper's mate. "No. While I wasn't positive at the time I met her, this conversation with the two of them certainly brought home to me how much I'd been duped."

Marley thought about how they'd met there, thinking that the household was asleep. No one, he realized, had thought to let them know much in the way of details. Then that got him to thinking about his other brothers if the other women were their mates. Marley asked the couple with him.

"One thing at a time, Marley. We'll get this bitch fixed up, then we'll figure out the others. All right?" He kissed her on the nose again. "You're going to have to explain to me why you think that works to distract me."

"I was in the back of the barn, as I said. I was near the window but not standing in front of it. I think they might well have seen me had I been. But being in the shadows and with Danish there with me, I had a perfect view of the two of them and could hear their every word." He thought about it again and how it had been a real eye-opener for him. "Piper was talking about how she hated to wear maternity clothing and how hot she was all the time. Her mother spoke then." Marley told the story as if he was in the conversation with them.

"Who cares how you feel right now? What we have to be concerned with is how he's not made any advances toward you to mate and bond." Piper told her mom he probably thought she'd crush him. "Behave yourself, Piper. You need to get this man to take you so you can take him to the cleaners. Don't you remember Mom telling us that the Morgans are the richest people in the world?"

"She didn't say that at the end. Grandma told us how Morgan had taken care that Aunt Rachel had a place to be buried and that she'd visited her all the time. Don't you remember that part?" Piper had snorted then. "That does not sound one bit like the mean people she used to call them when she spoke to us all the time."

"Do you want to have the money or not? I'd think that in your condition, you'd not be so fucking picky." She said it wasn't her fault at all that she was having a baby. "Then how did you get that way, Piper? Did you fall asleep during sex education class? The last time I heard, it took two people to make a kid, and you always have been one to spread your legs wide when you wanted a good fuck."

"He was good." The two of them giggled before Piper spoke again. "I love money, Mom. And the things that it can buy for me. Pretty dresses and nice shoes. Oh, what I'd not give for a nice comfy pair of shoes right now. But anyway, all right, I'll get him to fuck me. Christ, it was never this hard when I was younger."

"Younger? You moron, you're only twenty-one years old now. A bit young to be so jaded about sex." They laughed again as

Meredith plotted against him. "Now, you're going to bump into him every time you see him. I don't mean for you to knock him to the ground. Unless he's naked, then you jump on that cock of his and ride him like a bronco if you can."

Marley looked at his brother and sister-in-law when he realized what he'd said to them. Telling them he was sorry got a wave from Veni, as if it meant nothing to her, and Leslie laughed, calling him a bronco.

"Have you had any encounters with her today?" Marley told Veni that he'd not been in the house since yesterday and that Piper usually slept until two or so in the afternoon. "I wondered why I rarely saw her. Meredith has been sucking up to your mom, now that I think about it. So they're double-teaming this thing to get you to bond with her. What I don't understand is why?"

"I might be able to help you with that one." Danish sat on the table between the three of them and asked if she could tell them. Marley nodded, and his faerie turned back to the other two. "They have taken out a great bet—no, not a bet, but a loan—and have lost. If they do not pay it back within the next two days, they will be taught a lesson. I thought they should simply be taught a lesson, but Lord Marley thinks they'll use that against him in the newspapers and media places."

"I can see that. She'd do it too." Leslie sat back in his chair and realized they were all speaking aloud. "Can they have spies around here? Christ, I never thought of that until this minute."

"No one will hear what we're saying. I took care of it." Marley knew there was a story to that but was too upset about Piper and her mother to ask. Tomorrow, he told himself, and tried to make himself feel like he wasn't the bad guy in all this. "This loan, I'm assuming it's not with a bank or any other lending institution?"

"No. It's a loan shark. Piper and her mother both have a gambling problem. Even when the odds are so bad there is no chance in hell of them coming out on top, they bet the house, literally, and lose everything. I think that is the main reason they came here, to see if there was enough money from their mom to pay things down at least. Paying the attorney's fees took more than half of what they were to get. Then on top of that, there was no home for them to live in once they arrived."

Leslie explained to Veni how the house and land had been so poisoned it had taken some time for it to be cleaned up enough to use again. By then, Mom had purchased the land, and Zippy was going to have a shop with a greenhouse put on it for another shop. This one would deal in Wiccan items to sell.

"Okay. Let me see if we have all the information. They came here in hopes of getting enough money from the will to pay down a bit of the money they owed. Then they were more than likely going to sell the land—overpriced, I'm betting—to someone and run with the cash. That part I'm guessing about." Marley said that was correct. "So they get here, find out that not only is there not enough money for them to do much with but the land has been purchased by the family to pay for the funeral of both the women. I wonder how they realized there were unmated men around that had money?"

"The newspaper ran that article about how Mom had a wealthy son who married and that there were still five that were unattached. I think it even ran a picture of them." Marley told his brother they had. "So they get here, see the paper, and decide that you need a wife to help you spend all the money."

"No, they were going to make sure I didn't live long after the wedding. I forgot that part.

I would have died of some sort of unknown aliment on the honeymoon. Which Meredith was going to come on with us. And it wasn't me that was their first choice. I don't know who it was, but one of the others who had already been picked by one of the other women that came that week." Veni asked him how he felt about this knowledge. "Relieved that I'm not married to her? Terrified I won't be able to fix this? I don't know. How would you have felt if the thing was about you?"

"I don't know either. You said you didn't know if she was your mate when she first came. What made you decide she was?" Marley, embarrassed now, told them that Piper had told him. "Again, I can understand that. There was a lot of shit going on about then. Okay, we have to make sure you're safe from them both. I wouldn't put it past Meredith to jump you and demand that you marry her."

"Christ, I never thought of that. I'll steer clear of them both. Should I tell Mom too?" Leslie looked at Veni, so he did as well. "She'll kill them both, you know that, don't you? I mean, she might ask them what they thought they were doing, but she'll still be jabbing the knife in their hearts as she does it."

"Maybe we *should* tell her." Marley asked Veni if she was joking. "No, not with your very life on the line. No, she needs to know so she can, I don't know, do whatever it takes to make sure her boys aren't hurt. And you would have been too, Marley. Even if they couldn't have killed you, they would certainly have hurt you."

Marley reached out for his mom and asked her to come to meet him in town. He was not just afraid of what his mom would do to the two women, but he felt like he was going to disappoint her in some way. Marley, like the rest of them, didn't like to disappoint his mom. It was like a huge tear in their hearts when she would give them that look.

As soon as she sat down, Veni launched into the story as to why she was asked to come in. Mom looked at him.

"I'm so happy you figured this out. I didn't want to ever say this to you, but I can't stand Piper, and her mother is the worst kind of evil creature I've ever had to talk to." He hugged his mom, then laughed when she turned to Veni. "We have to be smart about this, you and I. I don't want to involve any of the boys, or she'll say things about them that will make it difficult for any of them to be in town. Women like these two are bad news. What is it you have planned?"

As Veni talked about what she thought they should do, Marley was suddenly very afraid of Veni too. She had a mind like his mom— thinking the worst of someone until they proved differently, and a murderous way of getting rid of the enemy. Marley looked at Leslie when he said his name.

"How about the two of us go over to the building going up for Zippy? Neither of the women we're avoiding will go there because there is a great deal of work being done, and I've noticed that neither of them are willing to do much unless they absolutely have to." He stood up when his brother did. Hanna was coming in as they were going out. Carroll was waiting by the car for them. "I'd hate to be on the receiving end of whatever those three have planned. I mean, it is going to be a bad ending for those two no matter how you look at it."

Carroll laughed before speaking. "I'm thinking it's no more than they deserve. I do know that Zippy is Bailey's mate. I've been around the two of them, and they're trying very hard not to show that they're madly in love. I think it's adorable." Marley laughed at his older brother. "Anyway. I'm not sure about Allison.

She and Scout are out of town right now. They're buying some horses and cows to replace the ones that have gotten too old."

The building was going up quickly, thanks mostly to the magic Zippy was using to help things along. As they moved around the shell, Marley could see that not only were there hidden places along the walls where she could hide specialty herbs and such, but she seemed to have a good start on whatever herbs she needed to dry. He asked her how she was doing.

"Very well. I've a few design changes I'll take care of when the faeries leave for the day. They tend to want to help me too much, and I have to turn them down. It hurts my heart to see them like that, so I just wait until they're gone." Marley said he'd noticed that too, that they wanted to help a great deal more than necessary. "Veni told me that you're having trouble with your non-mate. Is there anything I can do to help?"

"They're having a meeting at the Dairy Island now. Mom is there too. I'm sure that if you want to help me, they'll welcome you." She smiled and asked him if he needed help. The others had their end under control. "Thank you, but no. I'm doing all right. Thank you for asking, though."

"You're a good man, Marley. I hope you find a woman that will tell you that daily." He thanked her again and found himself embarrassed once again. "I do have a favor to ask of you. Morgan told me you did the best searches on things that were hard to find. I'm looking for a list of herbs that aren't around here. The faeries told me that if I could get them some seeds, they'd make sure they would grow, but I'm not even sure how to start a search like that."

"If you have the list, I can get back to you tomorrow about it. It'll give me a reason not to leave the house until this is finished." She handed him the list of about thirty plants. "I can tell you right now that two of these are at the house. They've not been planted yet, but there are a few hundred of the seeds."

"That's wonderful." He marked those off the list, and a few more he knew were around but hidden away too. "My goodness. If you keep this up, I'll have all I need before you leave, and you'll not have that excuse you need."

"Hello, darling." Roman kissed his daughter on the cheek and shook his hand. Marley was glad to know that the other man was feeling so much better. "Your mom and I were headed this way when we saw that you had already started the shop. It's going well then?"

"Yes. And Marley is going to be able to find me some seeds I want to grow too. Morgan is going to give me a plot of land to use so they'll be protected from others wandering around here."

As they spoke about the gardens and the shop, Marley saw his mom talking to Piper. It didn't seem to be a shouting match, but he kept an eye on them while keeping out of sight. When Piper walked away with a huge grin on her face, Mom turned to where he was and winked at him. He didn't think this was going to go on much longer if his mom and the other women were involved. And suddenly, Marley felt like the weight of the world was off his shoulders.

~*~

Leslie didn't have anything to add to what was going on in the courtroom today, but he was glad he'd gone. Rebecca was chained to the table, as she well should have been, and telling the judge, the Honorable George Tate, her version of the happenings the day that her family ended up in the river. Not one word of it was true, and Tate seemed to know that. It wasn't until Hanna stood up that things started to go better.

"You'll stop these lies this minute and tell the whole truth and nothing but the truth." She sat back down and smiled. Again, Leslie was sure he was more terrified daily of his new sisters than he was of his mom. "Go ahead, Your Honor. There will be no more lies coming from her to you."

After that, it was Rebecca telling, in great detail, how she had not just plotted to kill her children, but that she'd also been drugging them — including her husband — when she wanted to get laid by someone with the knowledge of how to make a woman scream, and for some quiet time. Rebecca even went on to explain how she'd been killing people for decades, where the bodies were buried, as well as a great many other things that no one had asked her about.

"I see." Tate looked at all of his family sitting in the courtroom. "I don't know what to do about all this information other than to do as you have asked me, Mr. Golden. I grant you and your wife full custody of the Canavan's children. Also, I have the paperwork here that I can sign now to allow you and Veni to adopt them. Christ, this is a shitshow." The woman taking notes cleared her throat. "Milly, you've been working with me for ten years. I think this one deserves a little cursing."

"Yes, it does. But I was only trying to hold back my cheers for the kids involved in this." Tate nodded and looked at Rebecca. "Since we're being so honest, George, I think you should throw everything you can at her to keep her off the streets forever."

"Good idea." He asked Rebecca to stand up. "Rebecca Canavan, do you wish to have a trial for all the crimes you've committed, or can I just tell you right now that you're going to prison for the rest of your life? My way won't get you the death penalty, but you choose."

"I don't want to go to prison. And I don't want those people raising those kids. I'd rather see them dead than with the Golden family." Tate shook his head as he explained to her that what she wanted was a moot point, as he was the judge. "You're just as stupid as all the men I've killed. You more than likely have a tiny dick too."

"I'm sure that every man that sees you and hears your tales has a tiny dick. Now, I'm deciding for you. You will be sentenced to fifty years for each of the seventeen murders you committed. An additional one hundred years for each time you drugged your children." Tate started to write down his verdict even though there would be a transcript of it for him to read. "Life in prison without any chance for parole for the murder of your husband and attempted murder of your children on July tenth of this year." Tate shook his head. "There is just too much to go over at the moment. I think that with what I've sentenced you to, you're not going to be getting out other than in a body bag." The gavel came down hard, and Tate was out of the room before anyone could stand up.

Rebecca was dragged away, kicking and screaming about how she'd been cheated. Out of what no one seemed to know, but she was gone, and his family sat there. It wasn't until Tate came out of his little side office with his street clothing on that they started to stand.

"Here is a copy of the paperwork I said I'd give you. My secretary is taking it to the upstairs offices to have it filed right now." Sitting down, Tate asked him and Veni to have a seat. The rest of his family did as well. "You're a very close family, Leslie. More than that, you are the most respected family in the entire state. I'd be happy to say that the world would think you're a good family. In saying that, I have something I'd like to ask you. You can say no if you wish. It's the reason I gave you the paperwork first and told you it was being filed. I have several children in need of some guidance. Not all of them are in trouble with the law, but they have — for the most part have had a worse life than the three you've taken into your home."

"We'll take them." Leslie looked at his mom when she spoke up. "We'll do it. Whatever they need, we'll take care of them."

"You don't know anything about them, Morgan. What if I'm sending you the worst kind of kids?" She told him they'd work out or not, but they'd take them. "Thank you. You've no idea how much I'm going to be thanking you for this."

As he told them about the three he knew of right now, Leslie listened with only half an ear. He was mostly thinking about how his mom was not only opening her home and their magic to these children, but her heart as well. He wondered, not for the first time in his life, how he'd been so very lucky to have been her son.

As they were leaving the courthouse, all the paperwork on the first group of kids in their hands, Mom decided she wanted to build another home on the land that would be housing for educational purposes. As she'd been listening better than he had, she knew that most of the kids coming had not only been kicked out of school at a young age but that no one had been able to get them to do much of anything but be in trouble.

"We'll not call them trouble. We won't even refer to the paperwork we have about them, only to know a little about the children." They all agreed. "Good. Also, we'll each take turns with them. Mostly because we need to find a fit for them, and I think raising them as a whole will give them more love and understanding than they've ever had." They were headed back to the house when Mom told them the rest of the things she wished for the kids. "We'll not spoil them. I know we could give them everything they would want, but that won't help them either." As Mom went over the things she had on her mind, he was glad she'd done this.

"Morgan, whatever you wish to do is fine by all of us." Mom smiled at Veni and thanked her. "You've raised some of the finest men in the world all by yourself. It will be a piece of cake with all of us helping you raise these children."

"I hope you're right, Veni, but I have a feeling it's going to be a good deal harder to raise them than six shifters that haven't any idea how to be a man and a beast." They all laughed.

"Now to talk about Piper and her evil mother."

Mom told them all what she'd been doing in town today. That she'd spoken to Piper about welcoming her to the family. They were to have a lovely dinner Friday night, and they'd be able to make her wish she'd never met them.

"I'm sure you can understand that I can't give you all the details. I want you to be as surprised as everyone will be when things come out." Leslie asked Mom if there was anyone dead from this. "No. No murders, but there have been a good many hurt by them. They're worse than their mother if you can believe that."

"I do." Marley asked if Leslie was going to be all right. "I mean, I don't want them dead either unless that's the only choice there is for ending this crap."

"More than all right, son. And no, I don't think anyone will die from this." She looked at Veni, and his mate shook her head. "No, no one will die, and you'll be just fine. Now we have Rebecca taken out of the picture, which will give us plenty of time to get this one in the books as well. By the way, before I forget to tell you. George said there was no reason for us to think we have to adopt the children coming here. We're going to help them be adoptable. But if we should want to, like Leslie and Veni's children, he'll rush it through as well."

They ended up on the deck after dinner. There wouldn't be too many more days like this before the trees started to lose their leaves and the weather turned chilly. Personally, that was his favorite time of the year — all of them loved the change in season. It was then it occurred to him that Christmas this year, he'd have a family to buy for. Thinking on that had him smiling for the rest of the evening. He told Veni what he'd been thinking when she asked.

"Christmas? I've not even thought of Halloween yet, and you're into Christmas. You're not right in the head." But he could tell she was thinking about it now. "Does your mom go all out for the holidays?"

"Not for a very long time. I believe she will this year." Veni would go all out, too, if he didn't miss his bet. "Will Halloween be a big one for you and your family? I'm not sure what a witch does for Halloween."

"Me either. By the way, Dad is the grand warlock to my grand witch. However, when he retires, he'll turn it over to you. I'm not entirely sure what that will mean for you or what it entails, but he said he'd talk to you about it soon." He thanked her for checking. "You're so very welcome. I was — Leslie, is that a unicorn over there?"

The pair had had their twins and had come to show them off. Hanna was so happy she got to touch the little ones that she nearly forgot to see if his children could. Bethy was so excited she squealed a few times, but it didn't seem to bother the beautiful creatures. As they each touched the horns of the parents, they were given a little magic. How much, he didn't know, nor did he care. This was one of the happiest days he'd had in a long time, and he wasn't going to think too much about anything right now.

After the children were put to bed, he and Veni sat on their own deck and watched the stars come out. Tomorrow they'd have to get the kids' paperwork filled out to start school, but again, he wasn't worried. They were well adjusted and smart — he didn't see them having to struggle too much to catch up.

"What did you tell Wendy about her money?" Leslie told her he'd forgotten about it. "Your mom still has the check. Morgan told me she'd give it to me if I wanted it, but since Wendy had trusted her with it, she would hold onto it for her. I think that made your mom very proud to know that Wendy came to her first."

"I guess we'll see what she has in mind for it first. What do you think?" Veni agreed. "Good. No more worries tonight. How about if we go to bed and I make you scream several times before you ride me?"

"I love the way your mind works."

They went into the house, and he took her to the bedroom. Leslie was dismayed to find Bethy in their bed sleeping. Picking the little girl up, she wrapped her arms around his neck and kissed him there. Leslie thought it was the near-perfect end to the day. Now he was going to make love to his lovely wife.

Chapter 7

Morgan was excited. But then the entire household was that way as well. Today they'd have two more children in the house. Even after a tumultuous beginning, not only were they coming to the house, but they were going to be welcomed. It just took Carroll coming into the room for them to settle down and listen.

"Do you think they'll be all right?" Veni asked Morgan what she thought would happen during their trip here. "I don't know. I guess I'm an old mother hen, and I'm going to worry about them like I did the boys. I know I'll be all right after this group, but I'm so— A car just pulled in."

It wasn't a sound she was used to anymore, tires crunching in the drive. The smell of an engine. They had nothing here that would make that smell or sound, at least not as loudly as a car would. Racing to the front of the house with the rest of the family, Veni caught herself just before she pushed Morgan out of the way so she could be the first out. This was, after all, a big day for the Golden household.

"What do you mean, you don't have them?" Veni wished now that she had been first. Morgan was upset, as was George Tate. "George, you said you'd be bringing them here today. We're all waiting for them—"

"If you come with me, Morgan, I'll tell you what's happened. They're both…. I'm not sure what is wrong with them. I was called on the way to pick them up and told they were in the hospital. That's all I know for now." She turned to look at them. "I can take most of you in with me, but not all. We have to hurry. I have no idea why, but they told me to hurry in bringing their mother with me."

"Veni, you and Hanna should go with Mom. If there is a chance for magic to help them, you two would be the ones that can help." Morgan nodded at Leslie but didn't move. "Mom, go now. We'll get there as soon as we can. Hurry so that if you can help them you—"

"I'm afraid." Leslie pulled his mom into his arms and held her to him as she sobbed. Morgan had never cried in front of her before, and it tore at her heart like nothing had ever done before. "I'll be all right. Hurry in if you can."

They were in the large car and on the way to the hospital when Hanna finally spoke. Veni wasn't sure if she was making a joke or not, but it did break the tension a little bit when she did.

"I don't believe they make a car large enough to carry all of us around in, do you?" Morgan laughed and cried a little more but did shake her head. "Morgan, I don't want to upset you more, but I have a very important question. If you touch the young men, will they be immortal like us?"

"I don't understand." It was Veni who explained it to her. "I see. If they're badly hurt, as you said, in a permanent way, they'll remain so forever. Yes, if I touch them, they'll be like us. Immortal. I never thought of that yesterday when we spoke to them. Did any of you touch them?"

"They didn't allow us to. Remember?" Morgan nodded and looked out the window. "I don't know if we had if it would have made any difference to them today. I can't feel them.

Nothing."

"You mean they've passed already." Veni told her they could very well just be someplace she couldn't touch their minds right now, but yes, they could have passed away already. "They'll come home with us. I'll do something for them that I've never done before for any human. I'll bury them on the land. They'll be Jeremy and Robert Golden. Our family."

Veni had been told about Morgan's parents and how they had sold Morgan off to be raped by several men, then killed. It was the night Morgan had been saved by the big mother leopard, Golden Eyes. The biological mother of the men that Morgan had raised as her own. Then, in the best possible karma she'd ever heard, both of her parents died falling from the balcony from their bedroom when her father had tried to shove her mother to her death as well.

The hospital was unnervingly quiet this time of the morning. They were taken back to the room the boys had been put in, and it was obvious they had both been beaten badly — to death, as it turned out. Robert looked like his body had been run over by something, and his face was nearly unrecognizable as a human, much less a sixteen year old boy.

Jeremy was much worse. Most of the right side of his face was basically gone. His jaw had been broken and had been put in place with a neck brace. His ear, as well as his right eye, were gone, as well as most of his hand. The fingers on his left were also missing. The sheet that was covering him was soaked through with blood. Morgan stepped up to the bed, but she kept her hands locked firmly behind her back.

"Do you know what was done to them?" Veni nodded but then realized she couldn't see her, so she told Morgan she did. "Where are the people that did this to them? I'm going to kill them."

"They're all three in jail. Oh, wait a moment. One of them was killed just as we came into this place. Now they're down to two in jail." She asked Hanna how. "Her husband broke her neck when she tried to convince him that she needed to be home and not in jail. She wished for him to say he'd done it."

"Had he had anything to do with this?" Veni told her no, he'd not. "And the other person? What was their role in this?"

"Morgan, it's not going to help you—" She screamed at her to tell her. "The other man held them down while the woman ran over them with the tractor. The tiller device, or disc implement, was on the back of the tractor, and she used it as she ran over them. Three times."

"Christ." She looked at the man standing there and realized he'd heard every word they'd been saying. "I'm sorry. I didn't mean to listen in, but I think you have given me the information I needed anyway. I'm so sorry about the boys, Ms. Golden. I was told some things you might not have picked up. Robert was alive when the ambulance got to the house. Barely so, I was told. Jeremy wasn't. However, when they tried to save him, he blipped. I'm not entirely sure what that means, but they've hooked him up to the machines to keep him in the state he's currently in. Robert coded three times on the way in, and he too was put on a breathing machine, as well as everything else he's on now to keep his heart pumping. I'm not a doctor but an investigator, and I don't have a lot of the details you might need."

"Thank you." Veni knew the circumstances but didn't think Morgan could have handled much more. "Can you find me a doctor? I'd like to be able to let them rest in peace. More than likely the first peace they've had since they were born."

The man disappeared, and in a few minutes, a doctor was there. Morgan asked Doctor Slip if there was any way they'd be able to function at all and was told there were no brainwaves from either of them. Too much head trauma. Then Morgan asked if their organs could be used to save someone else.

"I'm afraid not, Ms. Golden. For the same reason. Trauma has been done to their bodies beyond what you can see here. Jeremy is missing most of his brain, as the machine or the tractor tire crushed his skull. Robert has lost too much blood, and the things done to him were beyond what anyone should ever do to a child." Doctor Slip cried as she explained. "I'm not supposed to say this, and I hope you understand, but I hope those people rot in hell for the rest of their lives. To think that we as a state let them take care of these children— I hate to think what other monstrous things they've done to other children that made it out alive."

"I'd like to take them off life support if that is possible. Judge George Tate gave me full custody of my boys here yesterday. If you need him to sign off on anything, I know he's still around." The doctor said she'd check with him. When she left, Morgan turned to them. "Veni, I want you to see about getting the man that killed his wife a good attorney. Not the family, but someone that will do a good job. Hanna, if you could please see if you can find out what it will take for me to bury my boys, I'd appreciate it. As soon as this is finished here, I'd like to…I'd very much like to spend the day with the kids. Do you know why they were killed?"

"Leaving the home they were in would mean they'd lose the income from them being there. Also, the state has been looking into complaints about the home and were deciding whether or not to keep them as a placement for children." Morgan turned so quickly that both she and Hanna backed away. "Don't hurt us, Morgan. Please?"

"I'd not…I'm sorry. Are you telling me that instead of taking the kids away from them before they started the investigation, they left them there while they figured it out?" Veni nodded. "Someone has to pay for this. You know that, don't you?"

Hanna smiled. It wasn't one that Veni would want to try and decipher, either. It was frightening. When she spoke, her voice was much too calm for her to think she was anything but one pissed-off woman.

"Those people who were notified about the goings on at that house should suffer. And they are. Nightmares of what happened to these children will haunt them for the rest of their lives. They'll have the same nightmarish things invade their dreams nightly that all the children had to endure until I say otherwise." Morgan asked if it would hurt them. "Oh yes. Not physically, mind you, but they will suffer. Not needlessly, either. Also, I'll make sure they are able to rest and be well sometimes. I wouldn't want them to be able to end their suffering too soon."

"Hanna, you're frighteningly scary." Hanna smiled at her as if it were some kind of compliment. Veni didn't bother telling her any different but let her believe whatever she wished. "I'll make a few calls now."

George showed up about the time the doctor returned. All the paperwork was signed by Morgan, with George as a witness. The rest of the family showed up and held their mom while the life support was taken off Robert and Jeremy. It was the saddest thing she'd ever witnessed in her life.

As soon as the machine that pumped blood to his heart was turned off, Jeremy flatlined. Not a flicker of any kind showed for the full minute that Morgan asked for them to wait. Robert was the same, the thin blue line never wavering as it raced from one side of the monitor to the other. It broke her in ways she would never have thought to have to witness the death of such young boys.

The next several hours were spent finding suits for the boys. A funeral home who got help from Morgan before said that he'd take care that the bodies were ready for burial as soon as she was able to get the permission needed to bury them on private land. Carroll told his mom that he'd ordered markers for them and had paid extra for them to be ready soon. By six that evening, not only were the boys ready to be interred, but the coroner's office had done all the work to determine the cause of death. Both deaths were ruled a homicide.

The funeral wasn't much. There would be something in the paper in a couple of days about how they'd been murdered, Veni was sure. But for now, they gathered around the little cemetery that held very old markers that were centuries old, as well as one for the large cat, Golden Eyes. The boys were laid to rest on either side of the feline.

"You watch over them, Golden. For me." There was sobbing from all that were in attendance when Morgan said that to the beautiful marker between the boys. "You make sure they know I would have saved them had I known. I am so very sorry. Tell them."

Morgan went to the living room where their children were. A few cats came into the house, too, from a litter that had been birthed earlier that summer. Veni had explained to Sammy and Wendy what had happened, and they were happy to hang out with their Grandma Morgan. When dinnertime rolled around, they stayed with her to have make your own pizzas, a rare treat for the kids.

"Do you think she'll be all right?" Veni told Leslie she'd be just fine. She just needed time. "Yes, I guess. My heart hurts for her. I asked her if she'd do this again, take on children, and she patted me on the cheek and asked me why I'd think she wouldn't. I'm glad. I think this will make her better at being a caretaker for them. At least more tolerant of them."

"I think she'll do better than that, Leslie. I think your mom will be a huge advocate for abused children in placement homes. I know she'll make sure that all the kids will be safe around here for sure." Leslie kissed her on the back of the neck as they stood watching the kids make their pizzas. "I'm going to have one of those pizzas, so don't be getting all frisky with me. I've never had homemade cheese before, and I need to try it."

"You *need* to try it?" Nodding at him, she made her way to the table and laughed when Bethy handed her a handful of cherry tomatoes. While she made a pizza with just cheese, Leslie entertained Bethy by pretending to eat everything she offered him. The glee of her laughter was just what they all needed.

The homemade mozzarella cheese was beyond delicious. It was the best thing she'd ever had on a pizza, and she decided right then and there it would be all she needed when it was make your own pizza night again.

~*~

Piper was feeling really good about herself. Mom had taken her to get some much-needed maternity clothing. The shirt she had on was so pretty she wondered aloud if there was a way she might be able to wear it when she wasn't big with a kid.

"More than likely. You've always carried around a bit too much weight. Not to mention, you're going to be nothing but flab when you pop that kid." Piper asked her mom if she was at all excited about having a grandchild. "Those words will get you murdered, Piper. I never wanted you, much less you giving birth to a kid that will be more than likely just like you. No, I don't want a grandchild. You're still giving it up, right? After you get that man out of your hair?"

"His name is Marley. And I don't know how I'm supposed to get him to marry me when I can't even get to talk to him. Did I tell you he's been mourning? Why? They didn't even know the kids that died." Piper huffed. "I don't understand why he couldn't just come and see me or let me go by his house once in a while. In fact, I think he still lives with his mom. I bet if I didn't have to kill him off for the money, he'd expect me to live there too. But this mourning thing? Mourning for two dead kids that would have been around all the time is just stupid if you ask me."

Mom looked at her. "You'd better be figuring out what you're going to say to him tonight when we get there. I don't care if he has to take you right there on the frigging table while we're eating, Piper. Just make him have sex with you so you can marry him." She didn't really understand the having sex part. Sure, she was horny, but why did she have to have sex with the man to have him marry her?

Donald had fucked her a great deal, and she was carrying his baby. Nobody had mentioned him marrying her. Not that he could have, she supposed. He was already married and told her flat out he wasn't paying for another kid. She'd even, with her mom's help, gone to the welfare office to get them to make him pay some money to her, and Donald had sent them a list of men she'd been screwing around with while she'd been seeing him. That, to her, was a dirty assed trick.

Rubbing her belly again, she felt the kid move under her hand. It made her sick to know there was another thing inside of her, and it was sucking the life out of her. Well, she had been eating really good since she'd figured out why she was late with her period and stuff, but the kid was nothing more than a parasite. Christ, she was never doing this again. Ever.

"We're supposed to be there at six for dinner. You'd think they'd send a car or something for us." Piper told her mom—again—that they didn't use anything that ran on chemicals. "Gas isn't chemicals, dummy. It's gas. Christ, you're stupider than your dad ever was."

Since she'd never met her father, she didn't

know how to respond to that. Her mother was as much a "hoe" as she was, someone had said to her once. Piper just liked sex. Why was there a problem with that?

Standing in front of a mirror was something else she enjoyed. Today, with her new clothing on, she looked like a lost child with one of those swelled up bellies, like on television. Piper smelled her armpits, then looked at her hair, and decided she could go one more day without taking a shower. Her long stringy hair had that nice slick appeal to it that she could use in her favor.

While braiding her hair, Piper wondered whether, if she had taken those prenatal pills, her hair would have been glossy like the pictures showed. But after two doses of the things, she decided the kid would have to do without. They had made her belly sick, and her mouth tasted like one of those iron pills she'd had to take as a kid.

"Are you planning to wear shoes? Your feet look disgusting, by the way." She looked at them in the mirror, knowing full well she could no longer see them by looking down. "When was the last time you took a bath? You smell too."

"I don't think they'll notice, do you? As for

my feet, they hurt all the time, and rubbing them is the only way I can get them to stop burning. Like they're on fire." She picked up the soda can and realized it was empty. "I'm powerfully thirsty, Mom. Can you go out and get me another soda? I need to lay down and put my feet up before we go there. I'm guessing we aren't taking a cab or anything like that?"

"No cabs are in town." She had figured that out the other night when she'd wanted to go out dancing. Sitting around in the hotel room made her antsy. She didn't like that feeling. "I'll call out there again and see if anyone could come and get us. Surely they have some kind of car they use to come into town. Wouldn't you think?"

Not saying anything about the gas again, Piper laid down. It felt better to have her feet dangle off the bed, and that was what she decided to do. They'd be puffier, but she could get on her flip-flops all right. Besides, once they got a look at her new clothing, they'd not be looking at her feet.

When her mom jerked her awake, she realized she felt sort of sick. Even getting up from the bed seemed to take her forever. Also, her feet looked to be about twenty times bigger than they were when she'd laid down. Christ, her mom was going to have a cow.

"Get up. They're sending someone to pick us up in ten minutes. It had better be that man, Marlboro or something." She told her his name. "Yes, whatever. If it is him, you make sure you shimmy yourself up against him. Men love that shit, and he'll be hard as stone before you get to the house."

She was feeling sort of sicker but didn't mention it to Mom. There wasn't time for her to back out of going either. Getting up, holding onto the dresser in the room, she made her way to the bathroom to pee. When she stood up, she felt dizzier than before and sat down again. Mom yelling at her to come to look at what they'd sent to get them had her holding onto things to get to the door.

It was one of those old-fashioned wagons, with horses in the front of it to pull it. The horses were huge too, like taller than her big. Piper stumbled her way out of the hotel room and had to go back twice more to pee and get her shoes. Not that she could put them on, but her mom insisted that she bring them anyway.

"Why didn't Piper's mate come and get us?" Morgan only glanced back at them without answering her mom. "I mean, they're going to be married soon, right? They should get to know each other a little better. At least I think so."

"You go on thinking that." Piper nearly laughed, but her belly was hurting her again. Even sitting on the soft haybale with a blanket over it wasn't helping her with her belly. "Are you all right, Piper? You look a little ill."

"I'm not sure." Her mom told Morgan she was just fine. Just overly excited. "I'm not sure how I feel right now. I'm feeling sort of out of it."

"I'd say that's a good description. When are you due, Piper? Soon, I'm betting." She told Morgan she didn't know, as she'd stopped going to the doctor when he yelled at her about something. "What did he yell at you about? The extra weight? Or the fact that you're a diabetic? You should be taking better care of yourself while you're going to have a baby."

"She's not a diabetic. I know that for certain. When she first went to the doctor, he said she was healthy but needed to rest more. Then the very next time, he claimed that not only was she putting on too much weight, but that she was going to have to rest more." Piper mentioned the heels. "Yes, she had fallen down, and he said she needed to stop wearing high heels. What the hell does wearing flat shoes have to do with having a healthy kid, I ask you?"

"Perhaps he was thinking of the child she's carrying and that a hard fall could hurt them both." They pulled up in front of the big house, and before she could ask for help getting out, Morgan leapt off the sucker and was in the back with her. "You're not well, are you? I'm going to have one of my sons come out and carry you into the house. Then we're going to have you looked over. You stink too, Piper. You smell like old clothing and dirty body."

"I'm sick." To prove her point, Piper leaned over the side of the wagon and threw up. It was nothing but liquid. A little blood too. The next thing she knew, not only was she laying on a big bed with her feet up in the air, but she had an IV in her arm, and someone was talking across the room. "Hello?"

The man coming toward her was one of the Golden men. She wasn't sure who he was until he leaned over enough where she could bring him into focus. It was Marley. He was speaking, but she had no idea what he was saying. She asked him to slow down.

"You're in labor." She nodded, not sure what that was supposed to mean for a few seconds. "You're also gestational diabetic. Do you know what that means?"

"No. I hurt." He told her he could give her something for the pain, but not much, as it would harm the baby. "I don't care about the kid. I was going to give it up anyway after I killed you off for your money."

On some level, she knew she was saying too much. However, she didn't care. Almost as soon as the medication was put into her IV, she could feel the pain in her back and legs take over her mind. It was that bad.

Piper was in and out for what seemed like forever. Once when she opened her eyes, there were several people standing over her with masks on. It was too much—the pain was killing her. Closing her eyes, she let herself drift off again when someone spoke about large kidneys. Or kids, she wasn't entirely sure which.

When she woke up again, she was in the same bedroom. Looking around, she saw Morgan sitting in a chair with the other two women she'd met when she came to see Marley. Looking down at her body, she could tell that something was different, but she was too busy trying to stay awake to figure it out.

"Piper?" She looked at Morgan when she

said her name. "Your babies are doing well now that they're born. You've had some complications, however." Licking her lips several times so she could speak, she asked Morgan what it was. "The babies, even for being twins, were very large. Since you didn't take care of yourself and get help, they should have been born several weeks ago. As it is, you'll never have another child."

"Good. I hate kids anyway." Morgan didn't say anything, but she could see the shock on her face. "I don't want it. I guess them. You can have them. Now I can have sex all the time and not have to ever worry about getting knocked up again. You take them. I was going to give them up anyway."

"You said that before. You thought you could kill my son and get his money." She nodded, her head feeling full of cotton. "You can't kill any of us, Piper. We're all immortals. I don't care if you understand that or not, but I will take the children. You've not even asked what they were."

"I don't care. Where is my mom?" She didn't say anything in the way of an answer, so Piper went back to sleep.

The next time she woke up, she was in a hospital. It even smelled like one. There was a man sitting in the chair looking at something on the little table in front of him when she asked who he was. An attorney, he told her, with the paperwork for the adoption of the twins.

"Yes, hand it over. I'll do it right now." A nurse was brought in to witness her saying and signing that she was letting Morgan adopt the children. "Where is my mom? I asked before, but I don't remember anyone telling me."

He didn't answer her right away. When he took the paperwork from her, then had the nurse sign it too, he sat down. She didn't care for the look on his face like he was happy with whatever he was about to tell her.

"Your mother is in jail. That is where you're headed after you recover from the birth." She asked him what they'd done. "Well, you've admitted, several times as a matter of fact, that you had plans to kill off Marley Golden. And your ill caring for the children has you in trouble with the child welfare offices too. Not to mention, there is a warrant out for both you and your mother for the murder of Donald Holloway. The father of your children."

"Mom did that." He asked if she had known about it. "Well, sure. I mean, he was a bastard and didn't have to pay me any money for having those kids. But I didn't kill him. That's all on my mom."

A female officer came into the room then and cuffed her to the rails on the bed. When she sat down beside the bed, the attorney stood up. She told him she'd changed her mind about the adoption.

"It's a bit too late for that. You have a nice life, wherever you end up." The man was laughing on his way out of the room.

No matter how many times she asked the cop if she could just let her go, she didn't say a word. This was nuts. What the hell was happening to her? When her dinner was brought to her, it was nothing but liquids. No sugary treats, no pop. On the list that came with her meal was the stamp that she was on a diabetic diet. Fuck this shit. When she got out of here, she was going to have whatever the fuck she wanted from now on.

Chapter 8

Leslie handed Rodney to Veni when he was done feeding him. Bailey was feeding Rachel, and Zippy was rocking the baby that had been abandoned at the fire station not an hour ago. Her name was Sara. They'd be leaving the hospital tomorrow for home, and then they'd be Bailey and Zippy's children.

"Mom is excited to have all these kids around her. When Carroll and Hanna have their baby, she's going to be crazy happy." Bailey smiled at him. "Are you going to need some help? Wendy and Sammy have told me several times that they'll help babysit for free for you guys."

"I'm sure we will. But Zippy's parents have volunteered to watch over them for us too.

Just about everyone in town who heard about them is putting their name in for taking care of them. Do you think I'm insane?" All three of them, including Zippy, said yes. "Well, that was rude. But I meant for taking on three infants at one time."

"Are you happy?" Leslie only had to look at his brother to know he was. "Then that's all that matters. It's going to be tough, I'm betting, but you have family around and plenty of hands in the faeries, so you should be just great."

The little faeries were excited to have babies around as much as Mom was. But they still loved hanging out with his three. They could talk to them, he was told, and that made it all the better sometimes. As they were finishing up with the babies, he and Veni decided to go get something to eat. Zippy and Bailey joined them.

"I was thinking about something a little bit ago. What happens to the paperwork that says Piper and Marley are married? I thought Carroll said it had been filed with your paperwork." He told him what Carroll had said to him. "I guess if we can have it put in the courthouse, it's just as easy to have it taken out. I'm glad. I think Marley is happy in the end as well. Yesterday I saw him flirting again. The man has no shame."

"That's what makes him so loveable." Veni laid her menu down when she decided that she was having one of everything. "I've been thinking about a couple of things while this was all going on. In addition to the work I'm going to be working on with my sister, what else do you need me to do? I'm not going to be idle, not that I think Morgan would allow that, but I need something to keep my mind in the game. One of the things I was thinking about was opening a law practice that would benefit children in abusive situations."

"I love that idea. I have a law degree as well." She smiled at him. "I guess you want me to be a part of it too. I'm game. What else have you been thinking about?"

"Several things come to mind." Before she could elaborate on what she had on her mind, Zippy asked her about the shop. "You and I will still run it if you want me to. I have no trouble with that. Dad wants to help too. But lately, I think he's been leaning more toward going to the elementary school to volunteer a couple of days a week. He said that would give him first-hand knowledge of what is going on there. Dad is worried that, like with Robert and his brother, things are being overlooked on the teacher level."

Leslie listened to the others talking, but he did take a look around the restaurant a few times. He could see that everyone was enjoying themselves and was glad that after the last few days, he was able to relax a bit. It was just about the time they were being served their salads when his mom reached out to him.

I have two things to tell you. One of them is that I love you very much. He told his mom that he loved her as well. *Second thing. This is really weird, but I was wondering if you have any of the powers Veni has. The reason I'm asking is, there is a couple in town looking for the grand witch. The police sent one of the men here to ask, knowing that Veni and her family are witches, but I don't have an answer. Now, I know you're asking yourself, what does that have to do with you having witchcraft, but I wanted to know to see if you can seek them out somehow and see what they want.*

I'm here with both Zippy and Veni now. Let me ask them. Mom thanked him. Leslie posed the question to the two women. It was Veni that did the search. He told his mom what she'd been able to find out. *They're having trouble with their coven. I had no idea those actually existed. Anyway, she said she'd talk to them tomorrow. Zippy said you were smart to ask about them. There are all sorts of people out there scamming their way into a place to kill witches. While she's not entirely sure what is going on with these two, she said she'd keep an eye on them. And she said to thank you.*

The rest of the night was uneventful, and he was glad for that. As they made their way back home — Zippy and Bailey were staying close to the hospital so they could feed the babies — he thought of Christmas again. It was going to be the best one he could have imagined.

He was just getting his computer booted up when Bethy cried, so he got up to get her. Veni was working on a layout for the garden they'd put in next year for the herbs for the shop. Picking Bethy up, he nearly joined her in crying when the big fat tears started rolling down her cheeks.

"What's the matter, baby girl? Did you have a bad dream? Did something startle you?" After changing her diaper, he sat down in the rocker in his office and rocked her. "You seem all right to Daddy. You do know I'd slay anything that hurt you or your brother and sister, don't you?"

She put her hand on his cheek, and he kissed it. Watching her watch him, he wondered what she was thinking. He wasn't even sure he wanted to know what a seven month was thinking.

"Did you know that I'm a big kitty? I'll have to show you sometime. Wendy and Sammy too." Bethy smiled at him. "Yes, you'll have him wrapped around your fingers too, won't you? I don't mind. He'll love you as much as I do. I was just thinking about the holidays. I wonder if you...no, you wouldn't have been born last Christmas, would you? We'll have to get some ornaments. I think we might have some in storage, but I wouldn't even begin to know where to look for them."

"Do you always talk to babies in the middle of the night, Dad?" It gave his heart a little bump whenever one of the kids called him Dad. Sammy sat on his lap, too, when he asked if he could join them. "I don't remember ever having anything for Christmas before. Not even a tree. We went to see some of the neighbors once, and they had a huge one. But Rebecca made them mad about something, and we were never allowed to go there anymore. Do you think that Mom will get us some clothes for Christmas or toys?"

"Both." Veni sat down on the floor in front of them, and Wendy sat down on her lap. They were a family, a picture card family right now. "I do want your input on what you want. Just so you know, I would expect both of your grandparents to give you too much."

"I remember one Christmas we had when I was really young." Leslie asked Wendy about it. "I don't know a lot about any of the people that were there. I think it might have been Rebecca's mom or something. She died right after that. But she had this pretty tree that was as pink as the Barbie boxes. It didn't have round balls on it, but shiny things. Swans and water fountains. There were blinking white lights that made the whole room look so pretty. She let me touch a few of them, but then she told me they were very old and that I couldn't touch them anymore. That seemed so mean to me. It was like giving me a gift then taking it away. But I loved being in the house. Like this one, it was forever warm and clean. I'd forgotten what it was like to have clean sheets on my bed and a towel that I'm the only one that has used it." Leslie only had to glance at Veni to know that Wendy's innocent words of petty actions hurt her. "I'm so glad we're here with you. Not just for the things I said, but it's so nice to have someone hug you when you need it. Even when you don't. And Grandma Vicki is showing me how to cross-stitch, too."

"She tried to show me how to do that once. I failed miserably. She gave up after only a few tries. Zippy is good at it, though. Or she used to be." Wendy said she'd ask her then. "I have an idea about ornaments for our tree this year. Why don't we make them? There are lots of things around here that we could reuse. And I'm sure we can find things on the Internet that we can try as well."

"Can we bake all kinds of cookies?" Leslie told them how his mom was famous for her cookies. "Good, she'll let us cook with her. Grandma Vicki said she doesn't cook at all. I saw her making popcorn the other day, and she burnt it to smithereens. Yuck. The apartment smelled terrible all the rest of the night."

"We need to get your parents closer to us." Veni said they might move now that Zippy had three babies. "Good. I'd even pay for a house to be built for them if they would come to live nearby. I know that Mom has been enjoying having them around."

"I love that I'm getting to know the three of them too. The funny thing is, I already feel like we've never parted." Leslie stood up with the now sleeping Bethy in his arms as the other two were taken back to their rooms. Leslie was standing over the crib when Veni came up behind him, wrapping her arms around his waist. "I love you, Leslie. So much it's hard for me to find the words to tell you."

Turning in her arms, he kissed her. "I love you too. All the magic in the world cannot convey my feelings for you." He kissed her again. "In a few more weeks, the kids will be going to school. What if we were to head out for a few days and take them with us? I don't know what we'll do, but just take a nice vacation and buy an ornament or two to remember it by."

"I'd love that." She asked him if he had any special places in mind.

"No. I'll leave that up to you and the kids. Even if you wanted to go camping or something, I think we can figure that out. There might even be some tents and stuff in the barn. Though now that I think on it, three kids, one of them a baby, might not be the best thing to do with a tent."

They planned for the rest of the night. They not only found a camper to pull but also a good deal on a pickup. The two of them decided they'd find a place to store the camper and truck that wasn't on the property. That way, they'd not upset Mom.

"You think she'd be that upset?" Leslie

told Veni he didn't know, but there wasn't any reason to park it on the land. "No, there really isn't. I love the fact that it has bunk beds in the back for the kids. Also, that little area they can sit at when they want to have some time alone."

The sun was coming up when he started making them breakfast. Mom came up to join them, and they told her what they were planning. She asked if sometime she could come with them. Veni told her she would be invited every time they left if that would get her out and about.

"I think I might enjoy that. I've not done any traveling before, only to help out once in a while. Flying makes me feel like I'm going to fall out of the sky, but I think I'd love to go camping with you." Mom laughed as she helped get the kids ready for breakfast. "I came up here to ask you about something, but I don't remember what it was now. It must not have been very important."

Mom fed Bethy, who was in a very good mood considering she'd woken up crying. Wendy was talking to her about her money and how she was going to buy herself a computer with it and bank the rest. Mom told her she should invest and that she'd help her with that. He'd forgotten that Mom had a sort of insider track on things to invest in.

"I'd like that. Maybe when I'm ready to go to college, I will have enough money to not just go to college but also to not have to work my way through it. I guess that's really hard to do." Leslie said it was, as that was how he'd put himself through college the first time. "How many times have you gone to college, Dad?"

"Too many to count, I think." He put another fried egg on Sammy's plate and laughed when he devoured it. "I think you might be bigger than me soon. We have the best eggs on the planet if you ask me."

The longer they sat around the table, the more relaxed Leslie was beginning to feel. Not that he was too terribly stressed right now, but he was feeling all of his years over the last few days. When the kids were ready to go, they headed to the dealership to pick up the camper and truck. No time like the present to get the sucker loaded up and set out to parts unknown. Mom seemed to be excited too, and Leslie wondered if the rest of them might enjoy camping too.

~*~

"They're here. I can feel them." Connie looked at her mother when she huffed. "You could, too, if you got your head out of your ass and reached out beyond what the neighbors are up to."

"The thing is, I don't care that there is a witch around here. Nor should you if you know what's good for you. We've heard all over the place that she's the grand witch. And she has a grand warlock with her. Together it would be nothing for them to end your life if you fuck with them. I'm just saying, Connie, leave this alone." Connie rolled her eyes at her mother. "I'm going to have no part in this scheme you have going on in your head. And if you hurt me again, I'm going to seek her out myself and tell her what you're doing."

"You'll do no such thing." With a wave of her hand, her mother was lying on the floor. She wasn't dead—there were rules about killing off your family members. But since the witch across town wasn't related, she could do whatever she wanted. When her mother sat up, she stared at her for a few seconds before speaking. "How did you wake without me doing it? You're not that strong."

"No, but I am." Connie turned to look at the woman standing in her room. "So you have it in your head to kill me off, do you? Well, good luck with that. In the meantime, I'm going to take your mother out of here and put her someplace safe. The rule about killing your parents is very true. However, you're not supposed to use any kind of magic against them. You would do well, Constance Jamison, to remember that biting off more than you can chew will get you killed."

"I'm not afraid of you or your so-called grand witch magic." The woman said she wasn't the grand witch but her sister. "Sure you are. Then explain to me how you got into this room when I've used my considerable magic to make sure no one can enter without my permission?" The laughter rang throughout the room long after the woman and her mother disappeared. "Stupid bitch."

Going down to the basement where she practiced her spells and such, Connie knew something was out of place. The more she looked around, the more she realized everything she held dear was missing. Even the empty bottles she'd been collecting over the years were gone.

"Come to me now, you stupid cow." The laughter had her coming unglued. Reaching out to steal whatever magic was around her, she knew she would be able to bring the woman to heel and then kill her. "I command that you, Grand Witch, come to me this minute."

Nothing. Not even the dust down here stirred as she waited for her to come to her. Connie was stomping up the stairs when she realized she wasn't alone in the house. There were pixies all over her kitchen and living room. None of them looked like they were there for good.

"I should take the lot of you and pull your wings off and use it as magic." The laughter again. "What does she find so fucking funny all the time?"

"You, I would imagine. The mistress said for us to warn you once again to leave her and her family alone. We're here to make sure you don't harm anyone else in your ignorance. Also, you're not to harm any of us, or we can defend ourselves, so you don't try again. And you are ignorant, too, seeing how you think to take her on and come out on top." She flicked her finger at the one speaking to her and fell back against the wall. Her finger had been severed off to the knuckle. "You were warned to not harm us."

She staggered to the sink and began running water over the wound. Her finger was gone. Not just that, but the cut was so deep she could see the bones that had attached it to her hand. Wrapping it up so she could go to the hospital, Connie decided she was going to get the little fucker that hurt her. Even if he tried to cut her again, she'd be ready the next time.

The emergency room was busy. She didn't want to have to wait for someone to look at her hand, so she used a bit of magic to put herself at the top of the list. However, when the laughter rang around her again, she knew she was going to be fucked over with this as well.

You're not allowed to use your magic for the benefit of yourself. That's one of the first things they teach all new witches. She found herself sitting in one of the chairs at the far end of the department. *You are now at the bottom of the list, even below anyone coming in to check a sore nose. Sit there and think about what you're going to do with the rest of your life if I have to take all your magic away from you.*

"You can't fucking do that." She realized she'd spoken aloud and calmed herself down before speaking again. "You can't do that to me. I'm a great witch, and I'll be better than you too."

No, you won't. Sorry to tell you that so harshly — nah, I'm not sorry — but never. You're too stupid about your magic. Not to mention, from what I've seen in your mind, you've been warned a great many times about what you've been doing to others.

Suck it up, buttercup. You're going to be out of magic very soon if you don't get your shit together.

Connie decided to ignore the voice from now on.

It was nearly midnight when she was finally able to have someone look at her hand. It hadn't occurred to her to bring the finger with her, but the nurse told her it had been too long anyway, without it being put on ice, to attach it again. As the nurse tisked about her story as to how she had cut herself, she decided the truth was going to get her locked up. When the doctor arrived some two hours later, Connie told him she'd cut it while making herself some dinner.

After X-rays and a tetanus shot, she was bandaged up and sent home. The only thing they'd done for her was to put four stitches where her finger had been and told her to be more careful next time. They'd not even given her anything for pain. And she was dealing with a great deal of it by the time she got home.

Every time she bumped her hand against anything, she would cry out in pain. Each time she bent her other fingers to open the door or turn a key, she would cry harder. In the house, she went to her room and carefully put her hand up on a pillow and closed her eyes. She was going to fucking kill that bitch when she found her.

So that you don't go calling the police when you find things missing, your mother has been compensated for the things you've done to her. In the morning, you're going to be evicted from your home, and she'll live there. Before you tell me I can't do that again, it's done. She has also emptied the joint bank account you had with her — why she put you on there when she's the only one working is beyond me. But you'll have to find yourself a job and a place to live. Connie knew her mother wouldn't do that to her. *No, she didn't. I did. She didn't really care all that much when I did it, but then you've been treating her shitty for most of your life, haven't you?*

"I don't want to talk to you anymore. I'm in pain, thanks to your little fuckers. And if you think I'm just going to walk out of my home, you're much stupider than I first thought." The voice asked her if she thought everyone was stupid. She used that term a great deal. "When it comes to being dumber than me, then yes, they're stupid. Why do you care what the hell I've been doing to my mom all this time? It's not like she cared."

Didn't she? Well, you might want to ask her if you ever see her again. Connie didn't really care if she ever saw her mother again. But she wasn't going to leave her with nothing. Not so long as she had breath in her body. *You do know that I can do that too. Take all your breaths away. Let me show you.*

Air was suddenly cut off from her. No matter how hard she tried to inhale, there was nothing. It felt as if she had a bag over her head and someone was going to kill her. Clawing at her throat, she was nearly dead, she was sure, when she was able to abruptly breathe again.

Lying on her bed, her hand throbbing from being knocked around again, Connie cursed the voice for over twenty minutes before she cried herself to sleep. Once she was sleeping, the dreams started.

Every misdeed she'd ever done to her mother was there in her dreams. Only it wasn't her mother being abused, it was her, with her mother standing by watching. Each time she'd hit her with something—a stick, a car, it didn't matter—Connie saw it. Felt the impact all over her body. Over and over, she woke up screaming in pain, only to be slipped into a dream state again where her mom was hurting her.

By the time she woke the next morning, not only was her bed covered in blood, but she was as well. Going to take a shower, she unwrapped the bandage and cried again. There was blood still oozing from the wound, and she had a feeling she'd bleed out before she could get anyone to help her.

The shower refreshed her, but she still felt like she'd been run over. When someone pounded on her door, she didn't even get up to see who it was. They weren't going to take her home, damn it.

The door opened of its own accord, and she watched as three of the biggest, burliest men she'd ever seen came into the room with her. Asking them what they wanted, one of them picked her up, chair and all, and sat her near the sidewalk outside of her home. This was getting out of hand, Connie thought.

"Where the hell are you, bitch? I want this to end right now." The laughter. Sick to death of its noise, she cursed the woman with every spell she could remember. Connie was still sitting there when a large truck pulled into her driveway, and her mother got out. "Mom. What the hell do you think you're doing? You're not going to be welcome in my house anymore."

She couldn't move. Not to get up off the chair or to move into the yard. It wasn't until her locks were changed while she was still near the sidewalk and the truck moved away that she could stand up. But she couldn't get to the house. Not step a single toe into the yard — she'd tried that several times before she had to pick herself up off her ass. Screaming for the bitch again, she got an answer.

You're going to regret this, Constance. You get well, and I'll meet you. However, I'd not plan on this being a good ending for you. She said she was ready now. *Well, I'm not. So get your hand healed, and I'll get back to you. But you'd better have all your ducks in a row. Because I'm not planning to fuck with you overly much.*

"I'm not going to with you either. I'm coming for you, and when I get you, you're going to regret ever meeting me."

She said she already did, and the connection or whatever it was slammed shut. Good, Connie thought. I can plan without her always in my head.

Without money or a place to stay tonight, she walked to the library and hid out until they were closing. But almost as soon as the lights were being turned off, someone pulled her out of her hidey-hole and set her out.

This shit was getting old. With nowhere to

go now, she made her way to her home again. Still unable to get on the lawn, Connie laid down on the sidewalk and closed her eyes. Tomorrow she was going to take care of this shit with her mother, then kill her. Connie was going to kill that woman too.

Before You Go...

HELP AN AUTHOR

write a review

THANK YOU!

Share your voice and help guide other readers to these wonderful books. Even if it's only a line or two, your reviews help readers discover the author's books so they can continue creating stories that you'll love. Log in to your favorite retailer and leave a review. Thank you.

AWARD WINNING, BESTSELLING AUTHOR

Kathi Barton, a winner of the Pinnacle Book Achievement award as well as a best-selling author on Amazon and All Romance books, lives in Nashport, Ohio, with her husband, Paul. When not creating new worlds and romance, Kathi and her husband enjoy camping and going to auctions. She can also be seen at county fairs with her husband, who is an artist and potter.

Her muse, a cross between Jimmy Stewart and Hugh Jackman, brings her stories to life for her readers in a way that has them coming back time and again for more. Her favorite genre is paranormal romance, with a great deal of spice. You can visit Kathi on line and drop her an email if you'd like. She loves hearing from her fans. aaronskiss@gmail.com.

Follow Kathi on her blog: http://kathisbartonauthor.blogspot.com/

www.ingramcontent.com/pod-product-compliance
Lightning Source LLC
Chambersburg PA
CBHW030224180626
46810CB00008B/2963